CRACK IN THE SIDEWALK

A car driving at him out of the night plunges L.A. private investigator Mike Faraday into one of his most desperate cases. Assisted by his secretary, Stella, he discovers that the car has already knocked down and killed a brilliant scientist, Professor Hopcroft. The Professor's daughter hires Mike to discover why her father was killed; his death was murder and differing groups are engaged in a power struggle for The Zetland Method. As Mike tries to discover what The Zetland Method is, corpses and hair-breadth escapes come thick and fast . . .

BASIL COPPER

◆

CRACK IN THE SIDEWALK

Complete and Unabridged

LINFORD
Leicester

First published in Great Britain

First Linford Edition
published 1997

Copyright © 1976 by Basil Copper

British Library CIP Data

Copper, Basil, *1924*–
    Crack in the sidewalk.—Large print ed.—
Linford mystery library
    1. Detective and mystery stories
    2. Large type books
    I. Title
823.9'14 [F]

ISBN 0–7089–5065–5

Published by
F. A. Thorpe (Publishing) Ltd.
Anstey, Leicestershire

Set by Words & Graphics Ltd.
Anstey, Leicestershire
Printed and bound in Great Britain by
T. J. Press (Padstow) Ltd., Padstow, Cornwall

This book is printed on acid-free paper

1

THE car came straight at me out of the darkness, its headlights like two blinding white eyes. I just had time to get out the way before it slammed past. It was so close the chrome over the top of the near-side headlamp caught my sleeve and half-spun me round. I was on the sidewalk and still swearing before it had disappeared down the boulevard with a squealing of tyres.

It was about nine o'clock in the evening, a light rain falling and I'd come out to this section to see a man who'd phoned me in some trouble over his wife who'd disappeared. Like always the character wasn't in when I'd called at his apartment house. I'd hung around in my old powder-blue Buick outside but he hadn't showed.

I was just about to give up but

I thought I'd give him another ten minutes. I'd get Stella to write him off when I got back to the office in the morning. He'd probably made it up with his wife and forgotten to tell me he wouldn't be needing my services.

That was when I'd crossed the boulevard to get a package of cigarettes from a machine on the other side. I was coming back and had got about halfway across when the car turned the intersection and came straight at me. It was a big black sedan but naturally in that light I couldn't get the licence number.

Not that it would have done any good. The car was probably stolen anyway if I knew my L.A. A couple of kids most likely, high on dope and out for a ride and hoping to knock someone down before he could get clear. They scored fifteen points for a pensioner; thirty for an able-bodied person like myself; and fifty for another vehicle. I brushed myself down and grinned.

You're getting cynical, Faraday, I told myself.

That was when I heard the noise. It wasn't just the bleeping of the siren. You get those all the time in L.A. and my brain-box had learned to filter them out. But it was something like an angry murmur; the sort of thing you get from a baseball crowd when a strike has been missed. It came from somewhere beyond the intersection. I left the Buick where it was and walked on down the block, the neons shimmering through the rain, the gold,green and red reflections in the wet tarmac turning the roadway into a sea of fire. I lit myself a cigarette from the new pack, turning up my collar and shielding the match-flame from the wind.

I'd gotten to the corner by this time and I stepped round. The noise was coming from a large crowd of people on the sidewalk and spreading halfway across the road about a couple of hundred yards away. An ambulance was just nosing in toward the curb, its light winking, the howl of the siren dying away to a few mournful whimpers.

The stretcher party was easing its way through as I got to the edge of the group. They used their elbows as well as their tongues and the crowd started melting back. A crumpled figure was lying on its face, the hands in a pool of water. The hat had fallen off and tumbled white hair made the old man look like a crucified saint with his arms spread like that.

One of his shoes was off and lying a yard away from the body. Funny that always happens whenever there's violence; the shoes seem to be the first things that part company. The old man wore a white raincoat and the heavy score-mark of a muddy tyre went right along his body, running diagonally from his shoulder and down to his right ankle.

There was a murmur from the crowd as one of the ambulance men gently turned the old guy over. There was a lot of blood coming from the mouth and nose so I guessed he was all smashed up inside. The first man in the white jacket looked unemotionally at the other and shook his head.

"He's a goner for sure," he said in a dead, flat voice. "But we'd better get him in."

They started setting up the stretcher. I didn't know whether the old man was dead or alive but he sure looked bad. I was turning away when a big cop in a slicker gleaming with moisture started shoving his way through.

"What's going on here?" he said mildly, catching sight of the ambulancemen.

"Just another hit and run," the man in the white coat said.

The cop bristled and turned round, probing the crowd with his eyes.

"Anyone get the number?" he said. "Or see anything?"

The crowd started melting away. I went back to the Buick too and sat finishing off my cigarette. Then, because there was nothing else to do and because my client still hadn't showed I called it a day. I drove on home and hit the sack.

★ ★ ★

I sat with my feet up on my old broadtop and studied the cracks in the ceiling. The air-conditioning creaked in the humid silence and up in the far corner of the wall a big fat spider contentedly spun itself a web. All was right with the world. I grinned, conscious of the sticky patch of sweat on the back of my shirt. I put my feet down and glanced through the blind at the stalled traffic on the boulevard below.

The glare of the sun-shimmer off the chrome came up blunted by the smog and even with the windows closed I could hear the sharp note of klaxons and the dull roar of idling motors. I was throwing crumpled balls of newspaper in the general direction of the waste-basket when Stella came in.

"Second childhood again," she said.

"This is the latest line in psychological games," I said. "Backed by Edward de Bono and Dr Spock."

"My," Stella said. "You could have fooled me."

The gold bell of Stella's hair shone in the sunlight. She wore a simple flowered dress with a black belt which drew the thin material in over her flat stomach and emphasised her bust in a way there should be legislation against. It was too hot for that sort of thing today. She smiled as though she knew what I was thinking. Not that my thoughts were too subtle. Stella knew me better than that.

Her long legs were tanned and golden beneath the short dress and she wore no stockings today. She put down her bag and the copy of the Examiner she was carrying and went over to the alcove where we do the brewing-up. She put her head round the glass partition.

"I presume you're in the market?"

"Need you ask?" I said.

Stella grinned. She moved back behind the partition and I heard the snick of the coffee percolator going on. Nobody makes coffee the way Stella makes it and I was becoming like Pavlov's dogs whenever she was about to brew-up. I heard the clink of the cups and then Stella came back casually over to sit on her own desk and swing her legs and look at me with those frank blue eyes.

"What's new?" she said.

I shrugged.

"Just the usual hopheads driving automobiles over the bodies of complete strangers. I almost got the chop last night. And the guy at the wheel did get some old character. He looked pretty bad when the meat-wagon picked him up."

Stella looked at me sharply.

"Where was this?"

I told her and added a few more details for the hell of it.

"He died," Stella said quietly. "You're talking about Professor Hopcroft."

I sat up in the swivel chair and looked at Stella.

"It's in the Examiner," she said, flipping the paper over to me. She went on back over to the alcove again.

There was a fairly extensive downpage piece about the Professor. According to the Examiner it was an ordinary hit and run. Apparently he'd died an hour after admission to the General Hospital of internal injuries. I folded the paper to more manageable proportions and studied it while Stella brought the coffee.

Like always it was the best moment of the day. Stella smiled at my expression and went on over to the alcove to fetch her own cup. She came back and sat at her desk and stirred her coffee, looking at me thoughtfully. I added a mite more sugar and tasted the brew again. It was just right. I turned back to the Examiner.

Hopcroft had been sixty-seven and was an inventor of note; son of a Swedish mother and an English father he had come to the States in 1949. According to the paper he had lectured at various Californian universities and had carried on with his researches. His contributions to science had included the field of atomic energy and that of applied mechanics. He'd been on the board of the Malmo Institute in L.A. at the time of his death.

When I'd finished the report I lit a cigarette and sat smoking, frowning across at the boulevard through the window blinds, not seeing it, but merely the crumpled figure of an old man in a white raincoat with his arms outspread like a crucifix. Stella went over and switched on the plastic fan. The smoke clouds around my desk wavered and then dispersed.

"Sorry, honey," I said.

"I've heard of a brown study but this is ridiculous," Stella said.

I grinned at her.

"What do you know about the Malmo Institute?" I said.

"Nothing," Stella said, "But I can look it up."

"You mean to say we got reference books with that sort of information?" I said.

Stella crossed over to the minute section of bookshelves we run to, just below the large-scale wall map of L.A. which conceals the safe you can crack with a sardine-can opener. She ran a pink tongue round very full lips.

"We ought to have something to cover it," she said. "I bought several new directories last fall."

"Just so long as they come off our tax," I said, blowing a smoke ring toward the ceiling.

Stella came back tottering under the weight of a heavy blue bound volume.

"They do and they did", she said.

She slammed the book down on her blotter and looked at it enthusiastically.

"System, Mike," she said. "It's what you lack."

"That's what I pay you for," I said.

Stella smiled enigmatically and sat

11

down, crossing her long legs. I went over to pour myself another cup of coffee while she was doing that. I came back and took her own cup and re-filled that for her.

"My God," Stella told the filing cabinet. "The New Utopia is here."

"Just so long as you don't let the Women's Lib people know," I said.

Stella gave me another of her enigmatic glances.

"Who wants liberating?" she said cheerfully.

I ignored that. I went back to my own desk and carried on smoking and finishing off the coffee and admiring what I could see of Stella's legs.

"It's a think-tank, apparently," she said at last.

She looked up from the reference book and fixed me with very blue eyes.

"In what field?" I said.

Stella shrugged.

"Lots of fields. Applied physics. Electronics. Data systems. Transport

12

and aviation. Seems to cover almost everything."

"So Hopcroft taught at the Institute?" I said.

"Among other things," Stella said. "He was on the Faculty. And he carried on his experiments in the laboratories there."

I sat on in silence.

"You didn't tell the police about this, Mike?" Stella said.

"What the hell for?" I said.

Stella looked pained.

"Well, you were a witness, Mike."

I shook my head.

"I didn't see a thing. The old guy was killed hundreds of yards away from where I was, around a corner. I didn't even know it had happened until I heard the crowd."

Stella pouted. It looked good on her.

"You were almost run down yourself. That counts for something."

"Sure," I said. "I file a complaint downtown that a dark sedan, registration unknown, almost spreads my anatomy over the sidewalk. I'd look pretty silly looking in there. They must get a hundred every day."

I grinned at Stella's expression.

"I know you think I'm anti-social, honey. But it wouldn't do any good. If it would bring Professor Hopcroft back, sure I'd call in at the desk. But the age of miracles is past."

Stella shrugged again.

"Maybe you're right, Mike. But it does seem a shame. A useful man like that and no-one around to take the number of the automobile."

"Probably stolen," I said. "My bet is they'll fish it out of a harbour somewhere in about a month's time. And that'll be the end of it."

The phone buzzed just then. Stella picked it up.

"Faraday Investigations."

She cupped her hand over the mouthpiece and listened intently. The voice at the other end seemed to go on for a long time. She looked at me with

14

an enigmatic expression. Then she took her hand away from the phone.

"Certainly, come right on over," she said.

She put the phone down and drank the remainder of her coffee with maddening deliberation.

"It wasn't the end of it," she said triumphantly. "That was Professor Hopcroft's daughter. She wants to come on over and see you about his death."

2

THE girl sat down nervously across the desk from me. Stella smiled reassuringly at her and went to fetch some more coffee.

"You're perhaps surprised at me calling on you, Mr Faraday," she began diffidently. She had a husky, attractive voice that went with her close-cut ash-blonde hair and green eyes.

"I'm surprised at nothing in my business, Miss Hopcroft," I said. "I was sorry to hear about your father."

The girl looked surprised.

"You already know about it?"

I nodded.

"I was there," I said. "Not actually there but down the next street. The car almost knocked me down too."

There was a sudden silence, broken only by the faint clinking of cups from the alcove. The girl put a hesitant

16

hand up to the corner of her mouth. The gesture reminded me of that of a frightened child. She looked at me with suddenly trembling lips.

"You're asking yourself why I didn't go to the police?" I said gently. "The answer is that it wouldn't have done any good. The police get hundreds of hit-and-runs every year."

Some of the girl's colour was coming back now.

"I'm sorry, Mr Faraday," she said in that low, hesitant voice. "It was just that I was astonished at the coincidence."

I nodded.

"It struck me that way too when I heard you were on the phone."

Stella came back and put the big cup of black coffee down in front of the girl. Her eyes looked a question at me.

"Now that you mention it, yes," I said.

Stella shook her head slowly and went on back to re-fill my cup for the second time. The girl sat and stirred her coffee, her head down like she was

17

trying to read the future in the dark liquid before her.

She was above medium height with a voluptuous figure and a tanned complexion that bespoke perfect health; she was about twenty-five I should have said and there was something Scandinavian about her in the cast of her cheekbones; in the broad, smooth brow and in the sensuous lips and regular teeth.

Right now there was a darkness which hung about her features and gleamed out of her eyes. Despite her father's recent death she didn't wear any outward sign of mourning. She wore a flowered silk shirt with jazzy patterns of red and grey and she had a gold locket hanging around her neck which descended into the deep valley between her breasts.

She had a red silk jacket resting over her shoulders and a red matching mini-skirt. What I could see of her legs was sensational and she wore brown Cuban-heeled boots that must have been hot as hell this weather. She wore an ornamental dress ring with a big blue stone on her right hand.

The girl crossed her bare legs and cupped well manicured fingers round a shapely knee. I decided to help her out.

"I don't quite see what I can do for you, Miss Hopcroft," I said.

"Marion Hopcroft," the girl said. "I think there's quite a lot you might be able to do for me."

Stella came back and put the third cup of coffee down on my blotter. She went over to her own desk and sat watching the two of us, saying nothing.

"In what way?" I said, studying the girl. It wasn't too difficult. Especially on a morning like this. The girl put down her coffee cup with a faint chinking in the silence. She looked gratefully at Stella.

"It's nothing really that I can put my finger to, Mr Faraday. Just a hunch."

I shifted in my swivel chair and lit

another cigarette.

"I deal in hunches a lot in my business, Miss Hopcroft," I said. "But I'm not a mind-reader. It concerns your father, obviously . . ."

The girl nodded. She stared at me with a rather defiant expression on her face.

"I expect you're wondering why I don't show any outward sign of mourning . . ."

"Not at all," I said. "It isn't the Californian way. Besides, it's none of my business."

Marion Hopcroft shook her head.

"It has nothing to do with California. It was just that Daddy didn't believe in death. Leastways, the way those old people in the nineteenth-century did. He made me promise I'd carry on just as usual if anything ever happened to him."

Stella shot me a sharp glance. I stared down at my blotter and put down my cigarette on the edge of the earthenware tray on my desk.

"Is there any reason why anything should have happened to him?" I said casually.

The girl shook her head.

"Not particularly. But he was in some pretty secret lines of work. The Malmo Institute did projects for Government sometimes."

She broke off fiercely, as though she might say too much if she didn't keep close guard on her tongue. She picked up her coffee cup and sipped at it fastidiously before going on.

"Should you be telling me this if it's so top secret?" I said.

The girl shook her head.

"Probably not. But I shall never rest until I find out what's in back of all this."

I put the tips of my fingers together and leaned over toward the girl. Stella sat looking at us without saying anything but I noticed she'd already begun to take notes.

"Suppose you start at the beginning," I said. "All what, for example."

"You still don't understand, Mr Faraday," the girl said. "There's nothing tangible I can give you. Just wild hunches and suppositions. It's just that over the past six months of his life father had been under some sort of strain."

"That's easily explainable," I said. "Most scientists when they're working on intricate projects get that."

The Hopcroft number shrugged.

"Maybe," she said. "But Daddy was a person who never worried about his work. He was about the most phlegmatic man I ever came across."

"Was there anything particular you could assign it to?"

"Daddy almost never talked about his work," Marion Hopcroft went on. "But just a month ago he broke a rule. He said he had some problems. It was about something called The Zetland Method. I never told anyone, of course, and afterwards he regretted what he considered a breach of security procedures. He begged me never to tell anyone what he'd said."

"Despite the fact that he'd told you nothing," I said.

"Except the name of some process," Stella reminded us.

The girl's eyes were troubled.

"Does it mean anything to you, Mr Faraday?"

I smiled. I couldn't help it.

"I'm no scientist, Miss Hopcroft. I suppose we could check."

The girl almost got up from the desk in her agitation.

"That's what we absolutely mustn't do, Mr Faraday."

I looked from the girl to Stella and back again.

"In that case, I don't really see what I can do."

"You can start by asking some questions at the Malmo Institute," the girl said fiercely. "Someone there might know more than they're willing to admit."

I felt like an ant faced with the expanse of a brick wall. The girl must have sensed my attitude.

"I don't want you to mention The Zetland Method, of course. Not after what I've said. But an ordinary inquiry might start some hares. You see, for the last week of his life my father was a very frightened man. There was a strain in his eyes which I'd never seen before. And normally he was a person who didn't know what fear was."

She broke off and twisted her fingers together in her lap. There was a long silence broken by Stella who got up to fetch the girl another cup of coffee.

"What are you really saying, Miss Hopcroft?" I asked.

The girl raised her green eyes to mine.

"That was no hit-and-run driver, Mr Faraday. My father was murdered."

★ ★ ★

There was another long silence. The girl looked from me to Stella and then back again. There was a curious expression in her eyes, half-defiant, half timid. I decided to help her out.

"But you haven't got anything concrete to go on?"

The girl shook her head.

"Nothing but my instinct. If I had anything in documentary form I'd have brought it with me."

"It's a tall order, Miss Hopcroft," Stella said softly.

Marion Hopcroft looked at Stella with bright eyes.

"Don't worry, Miss Hopcroft," she said. "He's always like that at first. He'll take the case."

I gave Stella a steady look.

"You're being pretty free with my gaol-sentences," I said.

Even the girl smiled.

"Do you think something might be done, Mr Faraday?" she said eagerly. "Without, that is, putting yourself in such a position?"

There was something rather old-fashioned and endearing about the Hopcroft number; something that you

25

don't find in most women these days. I guessed it maybe had something to do with being with her father. Perhaps the scholarly atmosphere that surrounded him. Without knowing the old boy it was difficult to tell. But the image came back to my mind of him lying dying there in the gutter and the symbol of the crucified saint recurred.

"I don't know where we're going to start," I said.

I was talking to Stella but the remark was aimed at the girl.

"I might be able to help there, Mr Faraday," she said. "I could give you some sort of plausible excuse for calling at the Institute. Perhaps you could be a relative."

"Calling with the daughter's authority to clear his desk out," Stella said.

We both turned to look at her.

"Sometimes you almost justify your salary, honey," I told her.

Stella's eyes were a little frosty.

"I always justify my salary, Mike," she said.

"Do you always behave like this?" the girl said.

The expression on her face showed that she was in a world far removed from the one she ordinarily inhabited; despite her conforming dress I'd have said she was a girl who'd led a pretty sheltered life.

"Not at all," Stella said calmly. "When we're on our own we're twice as rude to one another."

I grinned.

"I suppose we'd better make some plans."

"You mean you will take the case, Mr Faraday?"

The girl's eyes were shining.

"He took it the moment you walked in the door," Stella said.

3

THE Malmo Institute was and is an eighteen-storey chrome and black glass block in downtown L.A. set back in five or six acres of landscaped real estate approached through an under-cover car-park complex. I tooled the Buick in through the entrance, drove up a ramp and slotted in behind a concrete pillar. Marion Hopcroft gave me a shy smile.

She already looked better than when I'd first seen her and in the clear, bright light she had a poise and alertness which hadn't been apparent in the office yesterday. Her green eyes were alert and sparkling and her ash-blonde hair was blown into tiny ripples by the breeze up here. We'd already rehearsed our routine so we didn't waste time on preliminaries.

The girl got out the car and waited for me to join her. She had the same outfit as yesterday but this time she wore the red jacket and she'd given up the boots for high-heeled black tan shoes. Her legs looked even more sensational than before. She looked like she knew what I was thinking so I didn't hang around out here.

We went up from the parking area and across a paved forecourt bright with tubs of tropical flowers to where the white granite entrance steps sparkled in the sun. Fountains were playing and the floor of the vast lobby was laid with polished afromosa so I guessed the Institute had plenty of money to throw around.

The girl ignored the large panelled reception desk with its three girls in white starched uniforms and led the way over to a teak elevator at one side of the lobby. There was no-one else around and the cage was already down so we got in and buttoned our way up to the fifth floor.

We got out in a broad corridor floored with cork tiles and with photographs of distinguished old guys with beards lining the walls. Up one end the passage was barred by a desk which stretched halfway across. A platinum blonde with a bright plastic smile which almost set fire to her uniform was sitting buffing her nails and pretending she was as busy as all hell.

She nodded distantly at the girl and reserved all of her thousand candlepower for me.

"Whom do you wish to see?"

"Professor Smithers," the Hopcroft number said. "He's an old friend of my father."

The blonde number frowned slightly. It only made her look a fraction less attractive. She opened up a green leather appointments book on the desk in front of her and looked at a sheaf of papers in the folder in back. She gave me a sharp look from under her lids and then bent over the papers again. She tapped with pink fingernails on a piece of printed pasteboard which looked like a duty roster.

"I'm afraid Professor Smithers is on leave in Europe at the moment," she said. "Is there anyone else could help?"

Both the girl and I knew that of course; in fact the Hopcroft number had been banking on it. She didn't need any acting to put a slight quiver in her voice. I put my hand on her arm.

"I'm Marion Hopcroft," she said. "Professor Hopcroft's daughter. You heard about the accident the other night?"

The blonde girl got up from the desk. She bit her lip.

"Oh, my God!" she said hurriedly. "Yes, we had heard about it. I'm so sorry. We didn't expect you down here today."

There was genuine sympathy in her eyes. I saw her looking curiously at the girl's jazzy outfit. I knew we had to act fast if we wanted to make out.

"Miss Hopcroft's naturally upset," I

told the receptionist. "And she doesn't want to drag this thing out. I'm an old friend of the family. Miss Hopcroft would like to clear her father's personal effects from his desk."

"That's his office just down the corridor," the girl interrupted.

The blonde number looked from me to the girl and then back again. Sympathy fought with duty in her eyes. Sympathy won.

"Normally we have rules about things like this," she said. "But I guess it'll be all right."

She hesitated, a pink flush suffusing the tan on her cheeks.

"I'll have to ask for proof of identity, of course."

"Surely," the Hopcroft girl said.

She opened her handbag. The receptionist was hunting in the desk. She came up with a bunch of master keys. She glanced at the documents Marion Hopcroft was showing her.

"It looks all in order," she said. "If you come along, I'll open up for you.

I'll have to report that you're here, of course."

"Sure," I said.

I thanked the girl with a big smile. She was already leading the way down the corridor. I figured we had fifteen minutes with a bit of luck. And who knew what the old man's desk might come up with during that time.

The key clicked in the lock. I noticed that the door was double-locked and that the blonde number had to use two different keys. I shot the Hopcroft girl a quick glance but she was already stepping forward into the office. It was a big room, painted white, with some good water colours on the walls.

The girl and I went on over the thick grey carpet. The sun was blazing through the big picture windows and it was hot and airless in here. The receptionist stood watching us for a moment and then she went over and started opening up the windows. The grey Venetian blinds rattled down, muting the glare and muffling the traffic noises which had suddenly become insistent with the opening of the casements.

There was a big cedarwood desk, some filing cabinets, shelves full of books behind glass. I suddenly knew there wouldn't be many personal effects. Seemed like Professor Hopcroft was meticulously tidy in all the things he did. The girl looked at me like she knew what I was thinking.

"We'd better make a start with the desk," she murmured.

The receptionist was staring at us as if she didn't know what to do next. She shifted her feet awkwardly. I decided to help her out.

"Is there an inventory or something?" I nodded toward the walls.

"The pictures for instance? Are they the Professor's or do they belong to the Institute?"

The girl looked at me gratefully.

"I'd have to take advice on that, Mr . . ."

"Faraday," I said. "We'll just clear

the desk. The ownership of any furniture or other stuff can be sorted out later."

The girl nodded, looking at Marion Hopcroft opening up drawers.

"That is something for the Faculty, Mr Faraday. I'll let the Director know you are both here."

"Sure," I said. "We understand. It's a responsibility."

The girl smiled at me winningly.

"I'll be just outside if you need me."

I waited until she'd quitted the room. She left the door open behind her. I looked thoughtfully across at it and set fire to a cigarette.

"You don't mind?" I asked the girl.

She shook her head. I put my spent match-stalk down in a big copper ashtray shaped like a wheel which stood on one corner of the massive desk. It was pretty bare. There were no papers, only a blotter, a desk calendar and an enlarged photograph in a gilt frame. I leaned over to have a look at it.

It was a study of the Professor sitting in a garden with the girl. It had apparently been taken a year or two before. The old man had a lined, sensitive face. The girl picked up the picture with a quick, convulsive movement and laid it face downwards on a corner of the desk.

I strolled over toward the door and peeked around it. The receptionist was lifting up the phone. She'd be dialling the Director's office. We wouldn't have much time now. I went back to the girl, closing the door behind me.

★ ★ ★

The girl was sitting behind her father's desk absorbed in her task. She had made a small pile of things; a faded snapshot of herself as a child in a plastic wallet folder; a bunch of keys; a theatre programme. The small debris of a life. I stood and watched her in silence for a second.

The girl looked up at me. Her eyes were suddenly brimming with tears. I went round the desk to her.

"It's all right," I said.

The girl got out a small scrap of handkerchief and dabbed at her eyes.

"I'm sorry, Mr Faraday. It just came home to me."

"Sure," I said. "Take your time. We've got a quarter of an hour or so."

I went over to a bookcase and stood frowning at the heavy volumes behind the glazing.

"You want me to look anywhere or do you want to do this yourself?"

The girl pulled herself together and became brisk and professional.

"I think I've got the personal things now, Mr Faraday. Daddy wasn't at all inclined to sentiment which is why it hit me when I saw this photograph."

She tapped the brown leather wallet that sat with the other stuff on the cabinet portrait.

"I understand," I said. "Suppose I take the right-hand set of drawers and you the left. Or are they locked?"

The girl shook her head.

"That's no problem. I got the keys from the police last night."

She was already leaning down, opening the drawers. I got down on my knees and riffled through the stuff. There wasn't much there, only a few cardboard files. I opened some of them up. They contained sheet after sheet of meaningless mathematical formulae. Meaningless to me, that is. The girl frowned as I showed them to her.

"We want something referring to The Zetland Method," she whispered.

I nodded. We worked on in silence for a few more minutes. It was heavy going and there wasn't anything which remotely resembled anything that might be on the top secret list. The girl went through the drawers on her side of the desk with calm efficiency.

There were a lot of printed documents in the drawers too. It would take time to go through all this stuff and time was something we hadn't got a lot of.

I found a sheet of impressive-looking

inked figures when I heard the whine of the elevator in the corridor outside. I got up quickly. I had an idea then. The girl passed me a long white envelope from a bunch in one of the drawers. I folded the sheet of figures and slid them into the envelope. I sealed the envelope and got out my pen.

I inked on the right hand corner of the envelope the single word ZETLAND in block caps and underlined it twice. The girl looked at me with a puzzled expression.

"Just bait," I said. "It might shake something loose if there's anything in the Malmo Institute to shake loose."

The girl smiled slowly. It was something worth looking at. I dusted my trousers and slid the drawers on my side shut. I motioned to the Hopcroft number to keep the others open. There were footsteps in the corridor. We waited, listening to the low, agitated murmur of voices from beyond the door.

"I don't care, you had no right,"

shouted a deep voice.

The girl looked at me quizzically.

"We sure annoyed somebody," I said.

I put the envelope on a corner of the desk with the single word facing outward, so it couldn't be missed except by a short-sighted octogenarian. I leaned on the desk and put my palm half over the envelope. I was still standing like that and the girl was making a big show with the drawers when the door burst open and three men erupted into the room.

4

THE tallest of them was a broad-shouldered man with a bullet head and his blond hair cut so close it looked like thistledown. He wore a well-cut grey lounge suit and he carried himself like he knew how to give orders. He had sleepy-looking eyes with long lashes and the lids were so close together he was in the room for some minutes before I could see they were a striking green-blue. He was about forty-five and had a strong face with a square jaw and square teeth to match.

His wide, horn-rimmed glasses made him look like the dynamic executive in the advertisements. I put him down as the top man but somehow I didn't feel he was the one who'd been doing the shouting in the corridor. He nodded pleasantly at the girl and turned his eyes on to me.

41

The second man was tall and thin and had a black beard tinged with grey. The mustachio on his upper lip was curled out widely from his head and made him look like a character in a French farce by Feydeau. The third man was smaller, with a neutral sort of face and sandy hair that was so long it hung down over his collar. He had an inflamed red face that looked like he was out in the sun a lot but couldn't tan easily because of his coloration. Both men wore long white coats like chemists.

The three men stood there looking at us for a few seconds and I could hear a noise like heavy breathing. Later I put it down to the bearded man's indignation. I could see the face of the blonde number looking in at the door. I stayed where I was and the girl didn't move from the desk, but just looked up at them as they came toward us.

"This is highly unethical, Professor," burst out the bearded man, looking from us to the blond man and then back again.

"I'll deal with this if you don't mind, doctor," said the big man in a bored, weary voice.

He suddenly smiled and opened his eyes, which transformed his face. He came forward, holding out his hand to the girl.

"We were so sorry to hear about your father, Miss Hopcroft. If there's anything we can do . . ."

The girl got up and they shook hands; the bearded man stirred himself like a dog that's been reprimanded and both he and the sandy-haired man made conventional noises denoting sympathy.

"Do sit down, Miss Hopcroft," said the man called the Professor smoothly. He beamed across at me.

"This is . . . ?"

"Mr Faraday," the girl said quickly, sitting down again. "An old friend."

"I'm glad to know you, Mr Faraday," the Professor said, giving me a hard, bone-crushing grip. "I only wish we'd met under happier circumstances."

He turned his blue-green eyes on the two men in the white coats. They shuffled their feet and made vague noises in the backs of their throats. I noticed the bearded character was giving stabbing glances all round the desk. The Professor hadn't missed anything either, but he was more subtle about it. He turned back to us.

"I am Professor Mackensen, Director of the Institute. This is Dr Eltz."

He indicated the bearded man who gave a stiff bow.

"Dr Eltz is Assistant Director," the Professor went on. "Dr Snell is third in the chain of command."

"The gang's all here," I said.

The sandy-haired man nodded distantly, opened his mouth, then apparently thought better of it. Mackensen smiled again and looked sleepily at me.

"You have, of course, every right to clear out your father's desk, Miss

44

Hopcroft. But I wish you had applied to me in the normal manner."

"It is highly unethical," Eltz snapped waspishly. He must have had a recording.

The Director gave him a warning glance.

"I'm sorry," the Hopcroft number said in a bewildered voice. She was getting quite good at this bit.

"I didn't realise we were doing anything wrong. I only wanted to get Daddy's personal things."

"Quite so," said Professor Mackensen quickly, daring the others to break in with a freezing glance from his eyes. "But much of the Institute's work is secret and we have to be rather . . . "

"Careful," I finished for him.

Mackensen gave me a disarming smile.

"Precisely, Mr Faraday," he said.

"I don't see where we've gone wrong," Marion Hopcroft said sharply.

She smiled at the blonde girl who had come a little farther into the room.

"The young lady was perfectly courteous and correct. We told her we wanted to clear my father's personal effects and she quite understood the reasons. But then a woman would."

The blonde girl smiled back at her and I could see small points of red standing out on the Director's cheeks. Before he could say anything the Hopcroft number was in full spate again.

"She already pointed out the things you've just told me. And there are just these few personal souvenirs of my father we wanted to take away."

She gestured at the pile of belongings in front of her. The bearded man opened his mouth then but he didn't get a chance.

"The young lady followed the correct procedure all the way through and rang you immediately. I think you owe her an apology."

Marion Hopcroft drew herself up and her extra-ordinary eyes flashed at the Professor.

"As for Mr Eltz' conduct I think it is not only heartless but boorish in the extreme."

I looked at her admiringly; she was doing a great job. The bearded man seemed to crumple as though someone had cracked a whip across his face. The sandy-haired man stood and said nothing. As before it was the Director who was the first to recover himself. He would have made a great diplomat.

"I agree with every word you say, Miss Hopcroft," he said softly. "Please accept my full apologies on behalf of myself and my colleagues. Of course it would appear like that to anyone outside the Institute. Your father would have understood. As Mr Faraday here says, we have to be very, very careful."

"Your integrity isn't in doubt, Professor Mackensen," I said. "But the manners of your hired help leave a great deal to be desired. I haven't heard Dr Eltz do any apologising yet."

The bearded man turned smouldering eyes on me.

"We're waiting, doctor," Mackensen said imperturbably.

He didn't look at me but had his eyes fixed somewhere up on the ceiling. The blonde number in the background was smiling now. Marion Hopcroft looked stonily at the bearded man.

"Naturally, you have my deepest apologies if I've said anything to offend at this tragic time," he mumbled.

Mackensen smiled, as though that settled everything.

"Well, that's better," he said. "And now, Dr Eltz I think it would be better if you left everything to me."

Eltz shrugged and gave the sandy-haired man a significant look. He stalked out with his head held high, brushing past the nurse, slamming the door behind him.

★ ★ ★

The sandy-haired man coughed. I noticed his eyes were on the envelope under my hand.

"Nevertheless, Professor," he said levelly. "There are security procedures involved here."

"Quite," said Mackensen, as though glad that someone was agreeing with him at last. "Let's all sit down. Perhaps the young lady would bring us some coffee."

"That would be fine," I said.

I went to sit behind the desk as the blonde number wheeled out. The sandy-haired man dragged a steel-framed chair over for the Professor and remained standing facing the desk. We were silent until the girl came back with four coffee cups on a tray and a plate of biscuits. I figured she'd been away about four minutes flat so they must have had a canteen somewhere on this floor. We were downing the coffee before Mackensen spoke again.

"There is a difficulty about some of your father's belongings, Miss Hopcroft," he said, turning to give the girl a sincere look. "For instance he was working on a number of projects for the Institute.

Then there were no doubt his own private papers relating to his personal projects. And finally the Government material."

"Which, it goes without saying, was top-secret," the sandy-haired man said.

Mackensen looked at him mildly.

"Just leave this to me, Dr Snell," he said.

Snell shut his mouth with a snap and glared at the ceiling. I'd never seen such a jittery crowd. If that was what it was like researching in the Malmo Institute I was glad I'd never majored in science. Their studies hadn't done their manners any good either.

"Just what is your suggestion?" Marion Hopcroft asked.

Mackensen stopped with his spoon poised over his cup.

"We have naturally no objection to your taking the material on the desk. And we have an inventory of other material, like pictures and furniture which belonged to your father. There's no problem about that. But I must insist that the scientific papers remain in situ until we have an opportunity to evaluate them."

"Just what happens if the Professor happened to have been working on a potentially valuable commercial process," I said. "Which was in his own personal area. And if that should be contested by the Institute?"

There was an acid silence for a moment. Snell seemed to turn a nasty shade of yellow and even Mackensen seemed caught off balance.

"I don't think I follow, Mr Faraday."

"I thought I'd made it quite clear," I said. "There could be areas of dispute. I think we ought to have this desk sealed until we get the lawyers in."

Snell half got up and then sat down again. I'd left the envelope on the desk in front of me and I saw him suddenly start as he glanced at it.

"Oh, come now, I don't think we want to take it that far," said Mackensen.

He was obviously ill at ease.

"You must see there could be difficulties," the Hopcroft girl said suddenly.

She was having a great morning.

"I hope no-one is doubting the Institute's integrity," the Professor said.

I shook my head.

"There's no question of that. But what I've suggested is just common sense."

There was another silence. Even Mackensen seemed nonplussed. Snell stood and fidgeted, keeping his eyes on my face.

"Have you any suggestions?" said the Professor, making an obvious effort.

"We could photostat the material and each take a set," I said.

The girl shot me a quick smile. The Professor shook his head.

"Absolutely impossible, Mr Faraday. That would mean you could walk out of here with potentially top-secret material."

"Looks like we got ourselves an impasse," the girl said brightly.

Mackensen frowned and I thought Snell was going to blow his top. I decided to put them out of their misery.

"I've got a better idea," I said. "We have the material copied but both sets are sealed. The copies go into a bank vault until the Institute has evaluated the originals."

Mackensen smiled. He ignored Snell's black looks.

"An admirable suggestion, Mr Faraday. If Miss Hopcroft could nominate a bank we will have the material copied straight away and everything can be sealed up in the presence of all of us."

He got up, rubbing his hands briskly.

"That's all right with me," Marion Hopcroft said. "I'm sorry it's come to this."

"It's difficult on both sides," the Director said smoothly.

I got up. The envelope was still lying on the desk. I knew the bearded man had seen it before he went out.

I wanted to see the reaction of the other two. I picked up the envelope ostentatiously and put it in my pocket. Snell licked his lips but said nothing.

Mackensen gave me a curious look. His eyes followed the envelope until I'd put it in my inside jacket pocket. He opened his mouth as if to say something and then shut it again. These boys were good at that. I patted my pocket and grinned at the girl. She finished off her coffee and stood up.

"If you'll get the photo-copying department on the phone, Snell," Mackensen said, "We'll make a start."

5

"**W**HAT do you make of it, Mr Faraday?" the Hopcroft girl said.

"It's an interesting situation," I said.

Stella smiled brightly. Her hair shone like spun gold in the sunlight spilling in through the blinds.

"From what I hear you almost overplayed your hand," she said. I shook my head.

"Miss Hopcroft did all right," I said. "I don't see what else we could have done."

Stella tapped with her gold pencil on perfect white teeth and frowned.

"Just what do you expect to come out of it?"

"Who knows?" I said. "Assuming Miss Hopcroft's suspicions to be right and with all due respect to her, they're only suspicions for the moment — we've made a move. Now it's up to the Malmo Institute."

Stella got up. "I'm making some coffee for myself anyway." I grinned. "The three of us will all think better on coffee."

Marion Hopcroft sat in the chair on the other side of my desk and looked at the little pile of effects in front of her. Stella had found her a big envelope and she was just putting the stuff away.

Stella clip-clopped over to the alcove and I heard the click of the percolator going on. I loosened my tie and stared across toward the window blinds, which hid the stalled cars and the smog on the boulevard below.

"It doesn't sound like you've got much, Mike," Stella said.

"You forgot one thing," I said. "It only took one phone call and the three top men in the Institute came running to make sure we didn't take anything from the Professor's desk until they'd had time to examine it."

Stella came back over toward us and shook her head.

"That sounds reasonable enough," she said.

"So it might be if one or even two had turned up," I said. "But not all the big guns, including the Director. There's something phoney there."

"You think so too?" the Hopcroft number said.

Her grey-green eyes were looking at me intently. The sun made dappled patterns on her ash-blonde hair, bleaching it to an even lighter shade.

Stella still looked dubious.

"You may have something, Mike. But even if there were some suspicious circumstances why should they worry, providing you haven't actually taken anything?"

"I didn't tell you everything, honey," I said. "I took a sheet of figures from the desk and put them in an envelope."

"And labelled it so that it looked

like it had something to do with The Zetland Method," the Hopcroft girl explained.

"I picked it up and put it in my pocket before I left," I said.

I took out the envelope and placed it on the desk.

"I made sure all three of them could see it."

Stella folded her arms and looked from the girl to me with studied patience.

"So you baited a trap," she said. "And did they try to stop you taking the envelope out?"

I shook my head.

"But if anyone there has a guilty conscience they might come after me. It's worth a try."

"It's your neck," Stella said.

She went over back toward the alcove. The Hopcroft girl looked alarmed. Her hand flew to the corner of her mouth again, making the gesture like a frightened child.

"I didn't think of that, Mr Faraday.

I do hope it won't put you in any danger."

"That's what I'm in business for," I said.

Stella came back then and put the coffee down in front of us. She went back to the alcove to get her own. Then she sat at her own desk and stirred the coffee, her eyes searching my face.

"If anyone had a guilty conscience there surely they would have stopped you taking the envelope?" she said.

"Not good reasoning, honey," I said. "One of them alone might be involved. He'd be tipping his hand to the Director if he objected. As well as calling attention to the importance of The Zetland Method."

I looked at the girl.

"Assuming The Zetland Method exists and it has any importance."

"It's a lot of assumptions, Mr Faraday," the Hopcroft girl said.

Her voice had a timbre of sadness in it. I'd forgotten it was only yesterday that her father had still been alive. She must still have been in shock.

"We'll come up with something," I said. "Would you like me to take you home when we've finished up here?"

"That would be fine," the girl said gravely. "What arrangements are you making?" I said.

"Cremation," the girl said. "It was in Daddy's will. The details are all fixed."

Stella put down her coffee cup with a tiny rattle in the silence.

"I don't know how you're set," I said. "But if you'd like somewhere to stay I've no doubt Stella could put you up a few days. If it helps . . ."

"Surely," said Stella, turning toward the girl. "I'm sorry. I should have thought of it myself."

The girl's eyes were soft as they looked up at Stella.

"I'm most grateful but it won't really be necessary," she said. "I have a staff back at the house and I'm pretty well looked after. They're going to do it tomorrow. I thought the sooner the better."

"Sure," I said.

The girl stood up.

"You've both been great," she said.

"I haven't done anything yet," I said.

The girl smiled.

"You know what I mean, Mr Faraday," she said.

I went over and stubbed out my cigarette butt in the earthenware tray on my desk.

"In the meantime we've set out the bait," I said. I looked at the girl.

"Next move is up to the opposition."

★ ★ ★

It was nearly five when I got back from taking the girl home. In fact I hadn't taken her all the way. She'd insisted on my dropping her off. She was going to take a taxi back. She seemed to think we might be under observation following the call at the Malmo Institute. It didn't make sense to me. But then nothing ever does in my business.

I parked the Buick in my usual garage and walked back to the building and rode up in the creaky elevator. The whole thing seemed pretty crazy. I was used to working on hunches but this was ridiculous. Marion Hopcroft was so convinced her father's death wasn't an accident. I'd said I'd play along but we had nothing to go on at all.

If the charade at the Malmo Institute didn't come up with anything I'd throw it in; in any event we couldn't take the thing on because there was nothing else to work on. I sighed. It had been one of those days. Thinking about the Institute reminded me of the envelope. I walked down to the office and let myself into the waiting room. Stella's typewriter was still pecking from behind the door.

She glanced up with a smile. I looked at her and shook my head.

"One more cup of coffee this afternoon, honey, and it will be

62

coming out my ears."

I got out the envelope from my pocket.

"Here's the bait. You'd better put it in the office safe just in case. It's the only bargaining counter we have. Such as it is."

Stella frowned. She got up and put the envelope away. Then she straightened the large-scale map of L.A. over it and came back to her own desk.

"A client phoned about an hour or so ago," she said. "He wouldn't say what he wanted."

I sat down at my desk and blinked at Stella. I lit a cigarette and put the match-stalk in the desk-tray.

"So?"

"So he said he'd ring back later," Stella said. "About now, in fact."

The phone buzzed as she finished speaking. Her eyes sparkled at the look on my face.

"Pretty impressive," I said.

Stella was already speaking into the phone.

"Yes, he just came in," she said. "I'll put him on."

I nodded to Stella and picked up the extension.

"Faraday," I said.

There was a short pause on the line. Then a rather flustered voice sounded in my ear. It was a man's, with a faint hint of a foreign accent.

"You wouldn't know me, Mr Faraday."

"Try me," I said.

The voice chuckled drily.

"I have a little business proposition to put you. One in which a reasonable fee for yourself would be involved."

"I'm always interested in reasonable fees," I said. "Especially where I'm involved."

Stella had her own phone to her ear; her pen raced over the paper as she took down the conversation.

The character at the other end of the line chuckled again.

"That's good, then," he said.

"You know my office," I said.

64

"Not so fast, Mr Faraday," the voice went on. There was a sudden sharpness which hadn't been there before. "I'd prefer to meet on neutral ground."

I grinned across at Stella. The man's hurried breathing sounded in my ear as he waited for me to go on.

"I'm agreeable," I said. "Providing it is neutral."

"What does that mean?"

"No bridges at midnight or graveyards around dawn. I've had some," I said.

"No, no," the voice went on hurriedly. "Nothing like that."

"Who is this?" I said. "I don't usually do business with disembodied voices."

"I'm afraid you'll have to be patient for a little while," the caller went on. "I'd prefer not to speak openly over the phone."

"It can't be that secret," I said. "If you don't come up with something sensible in the next ten seconds I'm going to put this phone down."

"Please don't do that, Mr Faraday."

65

The agitation in the man's voice was real; he almost yelped he was speaking so fast. This time Stella smiled across at me.

"What's the deal?" I said.

"You know the restaurant at Asti's?" the voice went on.

"Who doesn't?" I said.

"Could you be there around nine o'clock this evening?"

"How will I know you?" I said.

"Don't worry, Mr Faraday. I'll know you all right. I've taken the liberty of booking a table in your name. Number 24."

"You were pretty sure of yourself," I said.

"Until nine o'clock," the voice went on.

The phone went dead. I put it down and lit a cigarette. Stella put down her own receiver and stared at the mass of shorthand notes on the page before her.

"What do you make of that, Mike?"

"Not much," I said. "Ring Asti's,

honey, and see if they've got a booking."

Stella nodded. She pulled the L.A. Directory toward her. I got up and went over to the window while she was doing that. The snarled-up traffic on the boulevard outside didn't seem to have moved from the morning. I sighed. You're getting old, Mike, I told myself. The city's starting to get on top of you. I grinned at my reflection in the glass of the window. That'll be the day, I told it.

Stella was talking to someone with a very loud voice now. She held the phone while they went away to check. I sat down again as she rang off.

"He was right," she said. "There is a table booked. Number 24."

"Just so long as he's paying for it," I said. "It was a phoney voice, that was for sure. Sounded like the poor man's Charles Boyer."

Stella grinned.

"How would you tell?"

"I can tell," I told her.

I smoked on in silence for a few minutes longer.

"Anyway, we shall know more by this evening," Stella said.

I got up. "Maybe." I went and stood near her desk, looking down at her.

"You doing anything?" I said.

Stella shook her head.

"Nothing special."

"I thought maybe we could go grab a drink and a bite to eat."

Stella smiled. She stood up and put the hood over her typewriter with a quick flourish.

"I'd better say yes before he changes his mind," she told the filing cabinet.

6

ASTI'S is a complex of shopping areas, cosmetic parlours, boutiques and coffee bars with one main restaurant cantilevered out over a landscaped park with fountains and waterfalls. It was only a short drive so I didn't start until a quarter after eight. It was a fine night with a light breeze that took off the heat of the day and I felt almost happy as I tooled the Buick round the ess-bends that led up to the restaurant.

That mood wouldn't last for long so I savoured it while I had it. It still wanted a quarter of nine when I slotted in to the car-park and killed the motor. I could hear music and laughter coming from the restaurant and the lights stamped heavy lozenges of yellow on the tarmac as I walked on over toward the main entrance.

Frogs were croaking from somewhere, their harsh song cutting through the high shrill of the cigales and I could smell the heavy perfume of orange trees. I paused on the front steps, looking over the floodlit pool which had risen into view above the fringing trees. There were people walking along the paths between the trees and Chinese lanterns on flexes strung from the branches.

It suddenly looked incredibly phoney, like a film-set from The Great Gatsby. I grinned. You're too critical, Faraday, I told myself. I left the scene to the set extras and ran up the steps into the big stone and cedar lobby. There was a Soviet rear-admiral on duty at the swing doors who did his best to do me a serious injury by letting the door go at the wrong moment but I evaded him and went on down the lobby.

The orchestra had changed to a Strauss waltz now and I looked for Omar Sharif to show at the head of the stairs. He was slow in turning up so I went over to the restaurant entrance and gave my name to the captain of waiters, a surly, bald-headed character with a gold chain round his neck.

Gold teeth glinted in his mouth as he gave me a smile about five millimetres wide. He went over to a sideboard that was straining under the weight of trifle, ice-cream and similar stuff in silver dishes. He consulted a leather-bound register, turning over the pages with a flourish.

"Ah, yes," he said in a voice that reminded me of Peter Lorre in one of his more shifty roles.

"Mr Faraday. Yes, we have a booking. Table 24."

"I'm aware of that," I said. "I'd just like to get to the table and sit down."

He shot me a searching look from sad brown eyes. It didn't impress me. I've seen sad brown eyes on waiters before. They belong to some of the most ruthless men in the catering business. When they put the bite on you it's hard to wriggle out from under.

"You'd like to order now, sir?"

There was a slight pause between the last two words that was too deliberate to be an accident. I resisted an impulse to reduce the gold in his teeth back into its basic constituent.

"Who knows?" I said. "It depends on whether the man I'm meeting has turned up."

The sad brown eyes looked me over casually.

"You mean you don't know, sir'?"

"How would I, Horace?" I said. "I just arrived, remember?"

The captain of waiters gave a heavy sigh. The cracks in his personality were beginning to show.

"If you'd follow me, sir, perhaps we can find out."

"Great idea," I said.

Gold Teeth was already wheeling across the restaurant like his feet were on castors; the twelve-piece orchestra on the rococo rostrum at the back of the place was sawing away like mad now. Somewhere among the cacophony and the noise the fountains in the centre of the restaurant were making, I caught a snatch of One Enchanted Evening. They could say that again.

We skirted a pillar and found a table for four set against a massive column and skirting the edge of the fountain. If the wind was in the right direction one could get quite wet I imagined. But I kept the thought to myself. The waiter wouldn't have appreciated it. There was no-one around, just the four chairs leaning against the table, a silver centre-piece filled with tropical flowers and a white printed card bearing the legend: RESERVED.

The waiter frowned like someone had done him a personal injury. He consulted a gold wrist watch on his hairy wrist.

"The table was booked for nine o'clock," he said accusingly.

"Sure," I said. "That's why I'm here at five to nine."

The captain mumbled to himself under his breath and pulled out a chair for me.

"You don't want to order now?" he said softly.

"You're quite right, Horace," I said. "What would be the point. I'll just wait for the character who booked the table. He didn't give his name?"

Gold Teeth didn't quite sneer but he almost made it.

"You mean you don't know?"

"I wouldn't be asking you if I did," I said.

I was enjoying myself now; I sat back in the chair and looked around the restaurant. It was half-full but there was no-one around that I knew. The man who'd booked the table might be around, of course. He could be sitting somewhere nearby. It had been done before. Gold Teeth controlled himself with an effort.

"Would you like something to drink while you're waiting?"

"Bring me a cold beer," I said.

The captain's eyebrows shot up.

"A beer?"

"That's what I said," I told him.

The waiter's eyebrows lifted.

"A beer," he said to himself.

He flicked an imaginary fly off the table-cloth with a napkin and went off angrily, his back stiff, walking like he was treading on egg-yolks. I grinned and lit a cigarette.

★ ★ ★

I sat there for what seemed like a long time. It could only have been about ten minutes or so. The orchestra went on sawing away and I began to feel like I was in Old Vienna. Or Old Pasadena. It was that sort of place. All the time I was smoking and examining the decor I was casting my eyes over the clientele. I couldn't see anybody who fitted the bill for my caller.

There was a party of mannish-looking women with butch hair-cuts and raw, scrubbed faces at the nearest table, just the other side of the pillar. They looked like the faculty of a women's college having a night out. Judging by the uproar they were kicking up they probably were. Their leader, an imposing-looking woman wearing an incongruously low-cut dress and with mauve-tinted hair had a pretty good line in locker-room jokes, judging by the gusts of laughter.

Just beyond them was a girl and a dark-haired guy with a black mustache and hair down to his shoulders. They were so obviously wrapped up in each other that I ruled them out. There was still a desert of empty tables and the other characters I could see spread around didn't fit either.

They were mostly elderly or middle-aged parties or couples who were out for a good time. Or what passes for a good time in some sections of L.A. The captain of waiters came back in the end. They must have been short-staffed this evening because he was bringing the beer in person. Either my manner had impressed him or he figured I was too big a roughneck to let loose on his waiters.

He brought the tray in over the tropical vegetation with a skilled flourish and took the beer off with his disengaged hand.

"Lowenbrau," he said with what would have passed for a sneer in anybody else. On him it looked like one of those Round Table characters finding the Grail. I decided not to spoil his happiness.

"No sign of your party, sir?"

"Don't start that again," I told him. "I'll set fire to a table if I need anything else."

Gold Teeth gave a violent start, tortured his face into an amiable expression and went off with his stiff-legged walk. The orchestra went on sawing away at selections from The Student Prince while I started lowering the beer. As an evening it wasn't bad. Except that my man hadn't showed. It was half-past nine before anything else happened.

A wine-waiter with a key on a chain round his neck; a potboy; and a waiter with a bill of fare as long as a giraffe's hang-over showed up and made a lot of professional movements around the table. I figured that was another ploy on the captain's part. The skirmish ended fairly even; the wine-waiter retreated muttering and I ended up with another beer.

I shot another glance at my watch. A golden-haired number at a table in the middle distance was giving me the eye. She was about twenty and had cleavage that made Betty Grable look pretty flat-chested. I didn't follow it up though. She was with a character built like a prize-fighter and who had features that made Lee Marvin look pretty. There wouldn't have been any future in it. Leastways, not from my point of view.

It was ten o'clock now. I gave it up. I'd been conned. Question was, why. I got up and went over toward the restaurant entrance. Gold-Teeth was busy bowing so low to a group coming in he almost tore the carpet with his dentures. I didn't know Ronald Reagan was in town. I found another character with a granite face with a smile to match and paid for the two beers and the cover-charge. I felt like whistling when I saw the check but I paid it. There wasn't any point in kicking up a row. The table had been booked in my name.

I figured I'd take it out of the hide of the character who'd phoned me if I ever found him. I met Gold-Teeth at the door on the way out. He opened his mouth but I beat him to it.

"It's been a lovely evening but it had to come to an end," I said. "We must do this again real soon."

He shut his mouth in a firm, taut line and murmured something in his nostrils. He looked like an angry tortoise as he tottered down the restaurant looking for the waiter who'd given me the check. I saw a heavy altercation begin. It looked as though it might last the remainder of the evening if the two men worked at it. I grinned and went on down the steps.

I went out into the vestibule, found an unoccupied booth and phoned Stella at home.

"Nothing doing," I said. "It was a set-up. The character never showed. Just why, I wouldn't know."

I could almost hear Stella thinking at the other end of the wire.

"I've got no bright suggestions this time of the evening, Mike," Stella said, "Your call got me out the bath."

"Sorry, honey," I said. "You sure you wouldn't like me to come on over and dry your back."

"That'll be the day," Stella said.

She sounded happy though, the way she said it. I grinned again, told her goodnight and hung up. I looked at my watch as I got out the booth. It was just a quarter after ten. As an evening it was all shot to hell. There didn't seem to be anything else to do so I got the Buick and drove on home.

It was a fine, dry night now that

the heat of the day had gone and I enjoyed the coolness of the air. The traffic wasn't too bad this time of the evening and I made good time. I turned off the intersection.

I drove on over to my rented house on Park West and tooled the Buick into the car-port. I locked up and walked on over the cement path to the front door. I flipped on the light switch and snubbed the lock behind me. It was then I noticed minute scratch-marks round the edge of the lock plate.

They hadn't been there that morning. The lock was a slam-shut type. I opened the door and had a closer look. Someone had put a specially shaped metal instrument through and eased the tongue back. I slammed the door and re-locked it. I stood in the hallway looking at nothing. The house had that dead, empty feel that's unmistakable. Whoever had been in wasn't there now. I went over to the kitchen and flipped on the lights and then did the same with the living room.

81

There was a vase standing on the telephone table in the hall. The cleaning woman hadn't been in yet this week and there was the faintest film of dust on the top. Someone had moved the vase and put it back about half an inch to the right. If it hadn't been for the dust I wouldn't have noticed. I set fire to a cigarette and feathered smoke up to the ceiling. A real pro had been at work here.

I took off my jacket and went through the whole house. There wasn't a lot to see but now I knew what I was looking for it wasn't hard to read the picture. My caller had drawn me off for three hours while the place was gone over. The lock on my desk had been broken but in such a way that it looked accidental. I could have opened it myself and thought it was my own fault if I hadn't known what to look for.

Every scrap of paper in the place had been carefully sifted and then replaced. I walked through into the bathroom. Someone had even opened up the lid of the low level toilet suite and searched inside the cistern. There was a faint hair-crack showing now. Time was when I had hidden things there. I wondered whether to go on over to the office. Then I decided against. If the safe had been opened the person who'd done it would be away by now. And if someone wanted The Zetland Method they'd have enough technical knowledge to know it was just the Professor's random mathematical jottings in the envelope. I was beginning to believe the girl now.

I'd have Stella stash the envelope in the bank in the morning. That way it would seem like we had something to hide and would give us a bargaining counter in whatever game was being played. I thought about ringing Stella again and then decided to leave it.

I went back downstairs and cooked myself a meal and brewed some coffee. It wasn't the meal I'd intended tonight but I was starving by now. When I felt I might live with a little care and kindness I got out the L.A. Directory and looked up Marion Hopcroft's number. The girl came on almost immediately.

"Someone took the bait," I told her.

7

STELLA took the envelope out the safe and frowned at it. She put the map back over the safe and sat down at her desk. She looked at me without saying anything for a moment. I counted the cracks in the ceiling and listened to the creaking of the plastic fan in the semi-silence of the office. It was one of those mornings, hot and humid, when one longs for the mountains.

"What good will it do, putting this in the bank?" Stella said.

"None at all," I told her. "Except it's the only bargaining counter we have."

Stella put the envelope in her handbag and turned her blue eyes on to me.

"They may not just take the house apart next time, Mike," she said. "They'll probably start on you."

I grinned.

"I thought that was the general idea."

Stella leaned back in her swivel chair and gave me a long, hard look.

"I think we ought to get the police in," she said.

I stared at her incredulously.

"We'd be out of business in a month if we did that," I said. "You get this way at least once on every case."

Stella smiled, showing perfect teeth. It seemed to lighten up the morning.

"I was only thinking about you," she said. "Coffee?"

I nodded. I sat back in my chair and closed my eyes as Stella went over to the alcove and switched on the percolator. I listened to the faint chinking of cups, remembering the hundreds of times I'd sat like this in anticipation. I was getting more like one of Pavlov's dogs than ever.

"You think the phone man will call in again?" Stella said. I shrugged, opening my eyes.

"Your guess is as good as mine, honey. He might if he gets desperate enough. But whoever wants The Zetland Method might try the office next. It could be worth staking out the place. That's why I suggested putting the envelope in the bank."

Stella put her head round the glass screen.

"I'll take it down just as soon as we've had coffee."

She came back and sat on the edge of my desk, swinging a shapely knee. I shifted over so I wouldn't have to look at it.

"How that glittering taketh me," I quoted.

Stella smiled and slid off the desk and went back to the alcove.

"You'd better not forget the Professor's house either," she said, coming back with a full coffee cup.

I must have been a little dense this morning because it didn't register at first. Stella gave me one of her patient looks.

"The Professor," she said. "He must have had a study at his house. He probably did a lot of his work at home. He might have left some papers there."

I sat back in the chair and stared at her.

"Christ," I said. "You ought to be sitting in my place."

"I'm doing all right where I am," Stella said calmly.

I sat up and stirred the coffee. Stella pushed the sugar bowl across to me and tapped the lid of the biscuit tin.

"That was something I'd overlooked," I said. "I'll give the girl the word."

"Don't worry, Mike," Stella said. "You've only been on the case a day."

"Even so, it's something I should have thought of first time out," I said.

I lit a cigarette, putting the spent match in the earthenware tray on my desk. I took my first sip at the coffee. This was always the best moment of the day. Stella sat watching me, not saying anything, the sun glinting on the gold casque of her hair.

"You going to see the girl today?" she said.

I nodded, putting the cup down while I added a mite more sugar.

"I told her I might look over this afternoon."

Stella leaned back and clasped her hands behind her head. Her breasts looked so sensational when she did that I had to shift my position. It was too hot for that sort of thing this morning. Stella smiled faintly like she knew what I was thinking.

"Oughtn't you to warn her?"

I shook my head.

"I don't think there's any danger for the moment. Whoever took my place apart drew a blank. He'll either contact me again or try something else. There's a full-time staff at the girl's home, remember. It takes time to find a slip of paper or a document."

Stella folded her arms, assuming a less sensational position.

"I'd figure the girl's house is the last place they'd shake down," I said. "But you've got a point, honey."

I took another pull at my cup. Stella went around her desk, took the cup and went over to the alcove again. I leaned back and waited for the re-fill. She came and put the cup down on my blotter and slipped aside with the ease of long experience, evading my groping hand.

"Take it easy, Holmes," she said. "This sort of stuff will ruin your concentration."

I grinned.

"They want me all right," I said. "One of the three at the Malmo Institute got the point with the letter. That's why the decoy-stunt was pulled. But if they want to shake down the girl's home they've got to work undisturbed on the old man's study. That takes too much time."

Stella frowned at me.

"You're good at this sort of stuff," I said. "How would you do it?"

I reached over and took another biscuit. They were even better than usual this morning. Stella was a long time concentrating.

"We don't know how many staff the girl's got, Mike."

"Don't cheat," I said. "We can easily find out. For argument's sake, say housekeeper, cook and gardener. If you want to be extravagant, add a secretary for the old man. A total of five people, probably four."

I blew a smoke ring out and watched it ascend slowly to the ceiling in the humid air, hardly disturbed by the small eddies made by the fan.

"If they work at night, that means four or three — because the gardener will have gone at night. They'd obviously wait until the girl went out. That leaves two."

"And if the housekeeper had a night off, one," said Stella unsympathetically.

"I can't help it, honey," I said. "None of it sounds very good but I'm only theorising."

"They turn up as electrical repairmen," Stella said. "That's been done before."

I gave her a long look.

"You've been seeing too many TV series," I said.

Stella made a little face and went back into her thinking act. I finished off the coffee and pushed my chair back to give my feet more room to think. We weren't getting anywhere but it was passing the morning nicely.

"All we know is the Professor's dead; he had a theory someone may want; and that someone is interested because of last night," I said. "Hardly a lot to go on."

"But better than this time yesterday," Stella said. "At least we've got a case."

She got out from behind the desk and picked up her bag.

"I'll go put this in the bank," she said. "If you want any more coffee you'll have to make it yourself."

She paused and looked at me with very blue eyes.

"What are you doing about lunch?"

"Nothing special," I said.

Stella gave me a long, cool look.

"I'll buy you one when I get back from the bank."

"It's a date," I said.

Stella was still smiling when she went out the door.

★ ★ ★

Marion Hopcroft's place was a big spread up in the foothills and it took me nearly an hour to get there. I was still digesting Stella's lunch and the wine we'd had with it was making its way out as perspiration so I was glad to get up in the cooler air.

I tooled the Buick round the ess-bends, thinking about nothing in particular, watching a kite soaring over the far blue distance, the Pacific coming in in lazy white combers far below.

Way out the sea was shading to green and the sun burned as a brilliant yellow disc in the water. A sailboat with a muttonchop sail the colour of blood was breaking out a spinnaker and as I watched the big balloon sail filled with air as the helmsman put the tiller over and headed out toward the open sea. I sighed. That was something I never seemed to get time for. When did you last get down to Topanga, I asked myself. Certainly not for three years now. It's a tough life, Mike, I told myself.

I spun the wheel and turned on to a secondary road that seemed to go straight up the cliff. I was frowning by this time. I'd just thought of something. It was probably a small point. But small points usually add up to something significant in my racket.

It was just that the girl had had no car when I'd seen her yesterday. I'd ferried her to the Malmo Institute and had been halfway across town when she'd asked me to stop so she could grab a taxi. If she lived all the way out on Marina Bluff how did she get into L.A. Or had she stashed her own automobile with friends? Or perhaps her father had a house in L.A. as well as the spread out here.

I'd ask her when I saw her. Like I said it probably had a simple explanation but it was as well to check. That way we knew where we all stood. Marion Hopcroft had impressed me as a very nice little girl. But I'd known nice little girls before and they hadn't always stood up under close examination. I put the matter in a small reservation locker in my mind and changed gear again, turning the car's nose up another series of esses at the head of the bluff.

Anyway, the mental exercise passed the time nicely. I should be near the girl's place by now. That was when I saw the furniture truck half-slewed across the road. It had ZARCO stencilled on it in big black letters. I gave it a blast of the horn as it was veering round. It came to a stop half-blocking the road. There was a tan sport-job badly parked at the side of the narrow road a little farther on and I could see that was what had forced

95

the truck out. I drew up alongside and stopped.

The truckie's worried face looked out through the open window. He had hard, sun-burned features and brown eyes with very bright pupils.

"Sorry, mister," he said. "I didn't mean to give you a fright. Truth to tell, I'm in some trouble."

I got out the Buick and came up to the cab. The truckie looked down and started to open the door. He put his foot on the metal step and levered himself to the ground. He had on green coveralls over an open-neck shirt and he looked as big as a house.

"I've got some stuff here I'm supposed to deliver to a Miss Marion Hopcroft," he said, jerking his thumb in back of him. "It's supposed to be somewheres up on the bluff but I'm damned if I can see it."

"Coincidence," I said. "I'm going there myself."

The truckie looked at me incredulously.

"No," he said. "Say, ain't that something. We got no problem then."

He waved a grubby sheet of paper in front of my eyes, straightened it up against the hood of the truck.

"I got a large-scale here but I must have missed the lane somewhere."

I bent to look at the map. I must have been half-stupefied with wine-fumes. Or maybe it was just the sun and the air up here. It was the oldest trick in the world and I fell for it. I heard the faint scrape of a shoe on the road behind me. I half-turned when the truck fell on me and I went out and down into blackness.

8

THERE was a violent hammering noise and I was retching. I kept turning over in space and I was choking for breath. I shook my head then and found it was buried in sacking. I clawed up, my body shuddering and vibrations going through my muscles. The big truck crashed over the uneven road surface, the tyres screaming at the turns. Warm air blew through slats in the rear and bars of vivid sunlight stippled themselves across the flooring.

I knelt and waited for the little green men with the steel hammers to go away. My clothes were covered with dust and the inside of my mouth tasted of blood and old feather dusters. In equal proportions. I'd been rolled. My pockets were turned out and the linings hanging down. I knew then it wasn't an ordinary shakedown. The pro. after money just cuts the pockets out and checks the contents later. All my stuff was lying scattered on the sacking around me.

I found my loose change, my licence in the plastic folder, my note-case, my keys. Everything was there. I checked over the note-case, bracing myself against the bucking truck body. The bills in the case were undisturbed. I grinned. I knew then someone was still searching for The Zetland Method.

I looked back up inside the truck, clawing myself upright. There was a lot of furniture inside but it looked like junk. There was nothing but solid woodwork in front of me, separating me from the driver's compartment. There was nothing there. The rear door of the vehicle had slats in it; it looked like it might have been a cattle-truck at one time. I went up toward the tailboard. The slats were about two inches wide and I could see the strip of road unwinding behind us.

The Pacific still crawled below and there were villas on stilts dotted about the hillside. I figured I couldn't have been out more than a minute or two. There was no sign of another car behind us so I figured it was just the truckie and one other man. He would have been driving the tan roadster which had been parked at the side of the route.

I looked out through the slats, examining the rear flap. It was held by two steel pins on chains, shoved through the usual metal rings. They were kept in place by their weight. I went back in front of the truck then. There was a wash-hand stand there with a mirror. I looked a wreck. I tidied myself up and straightened my tie. I grinned again. Always the Immaculate Conception, I told myself.

I rummaged around in the drawers. Presently I came up with what I wanted. I took the long metal poker back to the rear and shoved it out through the slats. It might do but it was a heavy, unwieldy thing and the angle was awkward. If I missed I might drop it out on the road and I wouldn't get a second chance.

I got both hands round the poker and levered it inward, toward the pin holding the tailboard. The truck was bucking so violently it didn't matter how much noise I made; that was one thing to the good. The disadvantage was that it made precision almost impossible. I got the poker under the pin once but it slipped off almost immediately.

I found something out though. The weight of the tailboard was such that it held the pin stiff. To ease it out I needed something to take the weight off. I went back into the interior of the truck. I found a coil of rope lying on the floor. It was probably used to tie material to prevent it from falling. I figured the truck was part of a genuine operation. Most likely stolen for the job.

If that were so these boys wouldn't hang around. I figured that if anyone was interested in Professor Hopcroft's method — providing it existed — they'd want to question me. Especially if one of the three men at the Malmo Institute was involved; they'd seen the envelope and they'd want to know where I'd stashed it.

They'd searched my house and failed to find it; they'd searched me and found I didn't keep it on me. Aside from searching the Professor's own home, which might be complicated at this stage, they'd need to seek my co-operation. And that might be a painful process. I didn't want to be around when that happened. Leastways, not without the Smith-Wesson in my hand.

I took the rope and went back to the rear; the vehicle was still lurching wildly but the speed was a little slower now. I tied the end of the rope round a big stanchion near the top of the tailgate. I went back up front of the truck. There were rows of steel hooks in the bodywork, set at intervals, evidently for roping up tall pieces of furniture to prevent them falling.

I rove the end of the rope through the highest hook I could reach and carried it back to the tailgate. I shoved it round through the slats and tied it as tautly as I could, taking up the slack. I put the poker back through the space between two planks and found that the pin moved slightly when I touched it. All this had taken me over ten minutes. I might not have much more time.

I looked out at the ribbon of road spinning underneath. It still looked a pretty lonely stretch. At my third attempt I caught the underside of the pin a smart tap with the end of the poker. It shot into the air and fell free, rattling at the end of its chain. I went over to the left-hand side of the tailboard. This was a little more difficult. I'm not a natural left-hander, and even using my right hand I couldn't get the poker into the proper position very easily.

I tried for five minutes without any success. I felt sweat trickling down my face and dust driving in from the road was beginning to cover my clothes with white powder. I got hold of the slats then and pulled the tailgate up toward me, taking up the slack on this side. I made a wild upward swipe at the pin, felt the tip of the poker connect. Then it had fallen, bouncing on the road with a high, metallic clatter. But the pin was free and the tailboard sagged backward on the rope.

I thought I heard a shout from the cab above the rumble of the motor. Then the truck started to lose speed. There'd never be a better moment. I didn't stop to see what was behind, but freed the rope.

The tailgate went down with a shattering crash. Sparks showered up from the road surface as the metal staples dragged across it. I was already out the interior now, walking down the inclined plane. There was nothing behind me. I'd have to take a chance with traffic going the other way. The road looked like a white blur in the glare of the sun.

I rolled myself in a ball and threw myself down the slope on to the road. There was a roaring in my ears and a burning sensation in my shoulders. The sky and the road whirled round like crazy and I thought I was going to black out. I baled out right in the middle of a crossroads. I tasted blood again as I rolled over and came to a stop as a shrieking noise grew until it filled all my consciousness.

The big sedan was rocking straight for me down the side-road. Smoke was coming from the wheels, which were locked. It veered toward me as I tried to pull my legs round. Then it was on top of me and I blacked out again as it passed over my body.

9

WATER was running down my face. I choked and focused up. The big patrolman's battered face looked worried. Then he grinned as he saw me open my eyes. He corked the thermos flask.

"Jesus, buddy," he said. "Just what in hell were you trying to do?"

He shook his head mournfully.

"That was as near to Kingdom Come as I'd care to see this side of Thanksgiving."

I struggled up, his hand under my armpit.

"Did you see what happened?" I said.

My voice came out as a withered croak.

"You'd better take it easy," the big cop said.

I was still lying in the road. The

police sedan had passed right over me, its wheels still locked. I looked at the skid-marks on the hot tarmac in disbelief. The wheels had come within three inches of my legs at one point. I got up, found I could stand.

Another big guy, a younger one stood against the rear of the police car with a microphone in his hand. He licked his lips. Dark cheaters covered the upper half of his hard, tanned face. He didn't say anything. I looked back to the older character. He shrugged.

"We suddenly saw you roll out from the other side of the junction. Just where in hell did you come from?"

"It's a long story," I said.

I got out my licence in the plastic holder and showed it to him. The patrolman looked suddenly alert.

"I was rolled," I said. "A big guy who was driving a furniture truck. It had Zarco stencilled on the side of it. Probably stolen."

The second cop spoke through thin lips.

"We just had a call about that. Which way?"

I pointed. He nodded and took the microphone and went back to sit in the driving seat.

"You all right, Mr Faraday?" the first cop said sympathetically. "You look pretty rough to me."

"I'll live," I said. "I'd appreciate a lift toward town. I left my car parked a ways back."

"Sure," the cop said. "Be glad to. You'd best come in and sit out of the sun."

He opened up the rear door of the patrol car. I climbed in and he got in beside me. I suddenly felt groggy. I held on to the back of the seat. It was then I saw the condition of my hands where they'd torn at the road surface.

"Christ," I said.

"You see what I mean," the cop said.

I got out a pack of cigarettes, found they were squashed flat. I straightened one up and shoved it in my mouth. The big cop lit it for me.

"I was sapped," I said. "The truck was slewed across the road and I stopped to help the driver who said he was lost. He was a big guy in green coveralls with a hard face."

"Would you know him again?"

"Sure," I said. "I'd know him."

I smoked on in silence for a moment. The second cop went on rattling information into the microphone, in a flat, unemotional voice.

"The guy who topped me probably was driving a tan-sport-job," I said. "It was parked just a ways up the road but there was no-one in it. I didn't get the number."

The big cop relayed the information to the first man in the front seat, who clicked his microphone.

"You ever see this guy before or know any reason why anyone might do this?" the first cop asked.

I shook my head.

"When I came around I was in the

back of the furniture truck. I'd been rolled but nothing had been stolen. I let down the tailgate with a poker I found among the furniture and baled out. That's when I ran into you."

The big cop grinned.

"My, o my," he said. "What a dandy. Just wait until I tell my wife tonight. We ought to run you for being a dangerous pedestrian."

He chuckled throatily. I gave him a smile about three millimetres wide to show I appreciated his sense of humour. The first cop was off the radio now and started up the car. He turned it around and we set off down the bluff the way I'd come.

"Perhaps they wanted your car," the first cop said.

"They'd be welcome," I said. "I could get something better off the insurance."

The cop had his notebook out now.

"I'd better take your address, Mr Faraday, for the record. I shall need your signature for the statement."

"Sure," I said.

I leaned back against the car-cushions and closed my eyes. I told the cop my story in full. He took it all down with a stub of pencil. I opened my eyes again. He passed the sheet over to me and I signed it with my pen. He tore the top copy off with a flourish and gave me a carbon underneath. The driver turned his head briefly over his shoulder.

"They just found your furniture truck, Mr Faraday. About five miles farther down the bluff. There was no-one in it, of course."

"Of course," I said. "The two guys probably took off in the sport-job."

"Maybe it was in front of the truck," the first cop said helpfully. "What about the cab contents?" he said to the driver.

"Just coming through," the second cop grunted.

I closed my eyes again. We waited, the interior of the sedan heavy with static from the police radio.

"The green coveralls were on the

cab-seat," the driver said. "Apart from that, there was nothing."

I folded the statement copy and stashed it in an inside pocket. My hands were throbbing nicely now; the blood seemed to have dried. I stubbed out my cigarette in the tray in the squab in front of me and fumbled for another. The cop lit that for me too. I glanced out the window. I was beginning to recognise the landmarks now.

"What you need is a doctor," the cop said.

He looked at me sympathetically.

"Sure you can manage? You oughtn't to be driving."

"I'll see if the car's there," I told him. "I've got friends just along the bluff."

The patrolman nodded.

"O.K.," he said. "But if you want we can get you to hospital."

I grinned. It sat a little crookedly on me but it was a grin just the same. The Buick showed through the windscreen.

It was parked just where I'd left it. I tapped the driver on the shoulder and he slowed to a crawl and then stopped, keeping the engine idling. I got out. The first cop looked at me without saying anything. I went over and checked. The keys were still in the ignition. I went back to the patrol car.

"Thanks a lot," I said and meant it.

"Just part of the service," the first cop said.

His faded blue eyes looked like they'd seen a lot of mayhem over the years.

"If you've got any pictures you'd like me to look at," I said. "The L.A. boys know where to find me. I have an office downtown."

"Sure," the cop said. "We radioed the details in."

He held out his hand for me to shake. It was hard and dry.

"Take care, Mr Faraday."

The character at the wheel nodded distantly, his eyes invisible beneath the dark cheaters. I watched as they gunned out. I stood there until the dust had died away in the far distance and then I climbed heavily in the Buick. My clothes seemed to be in ribbons. Parts of my anatomy too. But maybe that was just illusion. I'd see just as soon as I could get inside somewhere. But for the moment the sparkle had gone out of the day.

I started the motor and then eased slowly out into the roadway. The traffic was light but I didn't aim to be involved in any more accidents this afternoon. I set off to look for Marion Hopcroft's place.

★ ★ ★

I didn't have to go far. There was a narrow lane about two hundred yards from where I'd been jumped. I turned off there, the Buick's springs protesting over the bumpy terrain. I drove up half a mile between flowering hedges, with the scent of orange groves in

114

my nostrils. Presently I came to a big white-painted five-barred gate. The gate was set back wide and pinned into a socket set into the surface of the tarmac driveway.

I idled the motor for a minute and sat feathering smoke through my nostrils. The whole of my body seemed to be on fire. In addition to the throbbing in my head there was a dull ache behind my eyes and my hands and knees were beginning to smart a treat. I hadn't examined myself too closely in case I fell apart but I could feel caked blood on my body beneath the clothes.

I avoided my image in the rear mirror. That wasn't good for my morale. I eased the Buick forward and followed the driveway which curved gently uphill toward a big white house at the top. The house had a green roof the colour of jade and the sun made sparkling reflections that winked back from the windows like diamonds.

There were the usual crescents of

well-shaved turf with sprinklers going; the statutory palm trees up by the terrace and the wide range of tropical vegetation that left a sharp, cloying perfume in the nostrils. Any other time I would have thought it great. This afternoon I was only functioning on one cylinder. I parked the Buick in a garage area at the foot of some steps and killed the motor. The chirping of crickets sounded loud in the thick silence.

I slid out the car and made it up the steps. The sun beat on the back of my head with dull insistence. I had a job putting one foot in front of another. I was more beat-up than I thought. Maybe the patrol car cop had been right. Perhaps I should be in hospital. I'd find out in a few minutes.

I got up on the terrace and made for the verandah that ran along in front of the house. There was a tall hedge with white flowers growing in it. Beyond the hedge I could hear loud voices calling in the warm air and the splashing of water. That would be the swim-pool area. Everyone had them up here. They were like tax experts and blondes; necessary equipment in California.

I got under the shelter of the verandah and out of the heat. It was dark and cool in here after the glare of the sun. I set my size nines along the tiling toward the porch. There was a double glass vestibule. Both doors were set open and the bronze image of a half-naked classical figure with a bow and arrow was propping open the inner one.

I couldn't find any bell so I went on into the hall which was light and high and even cooler than the verandah. My feet made tiny slithering noises on the polished parquet. There were gilt-framed mirrors on the walls and bowls of flowers set about on plain but very expensive-looking tables.

There didn't seem to be anyone around. I went on down the hall and found an ivory telephone on one of the tables; I looked at the dial. It was Marion Hopcroft's place all right. I slumped down in a deep carver chair and finished off my cigarette. I put the butt down in a crystal bowl on the table and dialled my office number. Stella answered straight away. Her voice sounded faint and far away.

I told her what had happened. She listened without saying anything. I figured she might even be taking notes.

"You all right, Mike?" she said sharply, when I finished. "You sound pretty awful to me."

"I'll be all right once I get under a shower and estimate the damage. I just thought I'd report in."

"Sure," Stella said. "What's your number?"

"I'm at Marion Hopcroft's place," I said. "I'll be in good hands."

"No doubt," said Stella drily. "Just make sure she calls a doctor."

"Will do, honey," I said. "I'll keep in touch."

I stood listening to Stella's closing remarks. I smiled and put the phone down. The thin thread of smoke from my stubbed-out cigarette was still going up toward the ceiling. I got up then, using my hands on the edge of the table. It seemed harder than I'd expected. I was still standing there when there was a sudden vibration along the hall and a smothered exclamation.

A girl in a white bikini, carrying a scarlet towelling robe stood by the mirror. She had a bronzed body that made Pygmalion's work look like a third-rate amateur. Water sparkled like dew on her perfect skin and her bare feet had made damp impressions on the parquet behind her. Her green eyes were wide and her ash-blonde, close-cropped hair shed droplets of moisture as she shook her head in surprise.

Her full lips opened to reveal the even teeth as she put a hand up to the corner of her mouth in a familiar gesture. There was compassion and something else hard to read in her eyes as Marion Hopcroft stared at me for a long moment.

"My God, Mike," she said, drawing in her breath with a shuddering movement of her breasts. Her flat stomach with the deep navel quivered.

"My God," she said again, in a low, dead voice. "What have I asked you to do?"

She held out her arms and I came into them. She held me close and tight against the coolness of her body as though she would never let me go.

10

I TURNED against the jet of hot water, the shower sluicing away pain, dust and weariness together. The soap made thick whorls of lather that eddied down the chromed grille at my feet. I watched them with almost sensual pleasure. I could see the silhouette of Marion Hopcroft's body dimly through the frosted glass screen of the shower-stall. She still wore the bikini.

"I still think I ought to get a doctor, Mike," she said.

I shook my head.

"I've inspected the damage. There's nothing broken."

"At least you should stay here the night and rest," the girl said.

"That I'll go along with," I told her.

I frowned at the deep gashes on my

knees, gingerly shifted the soap in the raw palm of my right hand. I'd been cracked up worse. I guessed it was the tap on the head which almost made me black out in the girl's hall. That and the heat of the sun after I'd left the patrolmen.

"I'll have Anna try and sew up the tears in your clothing," the girl went on. "She has a machine in her room. But I'm afraid you'll need a new suit."

"I've needed a new suit for years," I said.

The girl went and sat down on a stool outside the shower area.

"I'll take care of that," she said. "This was my fault. You haven't told me what happened yet."

"We'll go into that presently," I said.

I turned under the sting of the hot water and then switched to cold. The thin needles of the water and the iciness of the jets after the hot almost made me forget the pain. I stood it for a few seconds longer and then turned it off. I stood for a moment, letting the water drain off my body. The air was so warm I could feel my skin drying already.

The girl didn't say anything for a moment and I could see she was still sitting in the same position. I went over to the full-length mirror and inspected the damage. It was mainly confined to deep cuts and contusions on each knee; body bruising; and the peeling of skin from the heel of each palm. I'd been lucky. Apart from sundry other superficial cuts and a gash in one of the fingers of my right hand, that was all.

There was nothing broken and the headache from the blow on the head was dying away; I felt the lump. It was pretty big but I'd had worse in my time. I even started to smile as I gently towelled myself.

"You'll find iodine and talcum in the chest there," the girl said. "Or do you want me to do it?"

"I'd love you to do it, Marion," I said. "Only I don't know you well enough."

The girl chuckled.

"I trained as a nurse once."

"I can manage fine," I said.

When I'd dried myself I rummaged around in the chest and found what I wanted. There was no bleeding now. I painted myself as best I could. I couldn't help grunting from time to time and I could almost hear the girl's amusement from the other side of the screen.

When I'd finished I ran a comb through my hair and shrugged on the blue and white stripe towelling robe she'd left on a chair for me. It was a little on the small side but it would have to do for now. I guessed it had once belonged to the girl's father. Marion Hopcroft stood up as I got out the shower and came toward her. She looked at me approvingly.

"Just how I figured you'd look," she said.

She leaned up and kissed me gently on the side of the neck. The warm perfume of her breath seemed to go way down to my toes. She looked at me penetratingly; her eyes were a darker green now. I wondered why I'd ever thought she looked subdued in the office. She held out a pair of Moroccan leather slippers.

"They were Daddy's," she said simply. "Try them for size."

They fitted all right. I shuffled forward out the bathroom as she led the way.

"You're staying here tonight, Mike," she said. "You need rest and quiet for the moment. And I want to know what's going on. We're going to eat around half-past six. If you want a drink or some coffee in the meantime it's open house."

The girl led the way across the landing to a big balcony that was cantilevered out from the main house. It had glass screens all around but they were pulled back this time of year. There was a fine view of the surrounding real estate, the wide blue hills and the swim-pool on the terrace below. There were five or six people horsing around in the water. Their voices came up clear and brittle in the warm air.

"What about the guests?" I said.

The girl shook her head.

"I expect you think it queer that I'm apparently throwing a party after what just happened. They're friends and neighbours. They've come to show their sympathy. I figure it's better to carry on as normal rather than to just sit around."

I looked at her for a long moment. A light breeze ruffled her hair which was already dry.

"Sure," I said gently. "I wasn't implying any criticism. You seem pretty touchy if you don't mind me saying so."

Marion Hopcroft pulled down the corners of her mouth a fraction. She put on a white robe that was hanging over the back of a cane chair. I sank down into a long seat and lit one of my battered cigarettes. I drew in the smoke and figured I might last over the week-end with a little more of this treatment.

"I'm not touchy, Mike," the girl went on, tying the belt of her robe. "It's just that I care what you think of me."

I didn't answer that one but sat looking at the far hills and listening to the splashing water and the excited cries from the pool.

"Coffee or something stronger?" the girl repeated.

I pulled back toward her.

"Coffee would be fine," I said. "Black and hot."

There was a light step on the terrace and a motherly-looking woman with carefully coiffured grey hair, wearing slacks and a tan shirt came out on to the balcony. She was carrying a brown paper parcel. She cracked me a bright smile.

"Coffee right away," she told the girl. "This just came for Mr Faraday by messenger."

I took the package from her and waited until she'd left the balcony. The girl came over to sit near me, one bronzed leg showing in the opening of the gown. The parcel was addressed in Stella's handwriting. I opened it up. The girl looked at me with wide eyes as I took out the Smith-Wesson .38 in its webbing holster. I checked: there were five spare shells in the pouch like usual. I remembered then I'd left it in my desk drawer at the office.

I put it down on the floor beneath my cane chair and read the scribbled note Stella had pencilled: If you won't use your head, use this.

Marion Hopcroft cupped a smooth knee in her two hands and rocked to and fro, watching me with very cool eyes.

"She's quite a girl, Stella."

I nodded.

"Practical, too."

I finished off the cigarette as the housekeeper wheeled back with the coffee tray; she put the stuff between us and left without glancing at either. I waited until the girl had poured. She handed me the big earthenware cup. The coffee was black, scalding and made the way it should be. I closed my eyes and leaned back.

"You'd better tell me what this is all about," the girl said.

★ ★ ★

It had been dark for a long time. I was still wearing the dressing gown. It didn't seem to matter. She'd found me a pair of her father's pyjamas to go with the slippers and I felt almost civilised as we sat at opposite sides of the round table finishing dinner.

It had been one of the best meals I'd tasted for some while and I wanted to make it last. It was more likely to be hot-dog stands and more roughhouses from now on in. I'd had the girl stash the Smith-Wesson under the pillow in the bedroom she'd assigned me. There was no sense in frightening the hired help. The housekeeper came forward now and gave me another dazzling smile as she poured a second cup of coffee to accompany the cognac.

"It was worth getting knocked out for this," I said.

The girl smiled gently. She was wearing a dark blue shirt with a leather belt and tailored trews now but I was conscious of the magnificent body underneath. Too conscious for my own good. I kept remembering the bikini and the way the water had dripped from the gold of her skin.

"I have no secrets from Anna," she said. "You can talk freely."

"Just as well with me here in pyjamas," I said.

The housekeeper grinned but she was a pretty good diplomat.

"It's something that doesn't happen very often," she said gently.

The girl pretended to look shocked.

"I should think not," she said. "We'd better change the subject. How did you make out with Mr Faraday's suit?"

"I'm doing the best I can," Anna said dubiously. "But I'm afraid you'll look like something out of State relief."

"Don't worry," I said. "I usually get my clothes from the Red Cross."

Marion Hopcroft burst out laughing and the housekeeper looked startled for a moment before joining in.

"Well, they'll get you home all right, Mr Faraday," she said. "But after that they're on their own."

I thanked her and she gave me a warm glance before going on out with a conspiratorial smile to the girl. The windows were open and the croaking of frogs was coming from the garden beyond. Tiredness suddenly hit me as I leaned forward, drinking the coffee, the aches coming back to my limbs. Warm air blew in from outside, bringing with it the perfume of orange-blossom and I could hear the hollow murmur of the sea from around the point.

"A man could get to like all this," I said.

The girl's green eyes had a very intent expression as she stared at me.

"And why not," she said softly.

I thought it was time to change the subject. We'd already discussed what had happened that afternoon but there were still a few points I wanted to cover. I lit a cigarette and blew out the smoke, fumigating a mosquito that was doing a square dance on the cheese board. It flew off with an angry buzz.

"Stella made a point," I said. "About your father's papers. Incidentally, you didn't take a taxi out here yesterday?"

Marion Hopcroft looked startled.

"Of course not," she said. "I'd left my car in the driveway of a friend's house. We couldn't exist out here without transport."

"I just wondered if you had another place in L.A.," I said.

The girl shook her head.

"What's on your mind, Mike?"

"Something Stella said," I told her.

"She wondered whether your father had any papers in his study out here. Something to do with The Zetland Method, I mean. She thought we ought to take precautions in case anybody gets ideas about this place."

The girl shivered suddenly. She looked anxiously toward the window as though there might be someone out in the darkness of the garden.

"Don't worry, Mike," she said. "There's nothing here. Father didn't even have a study as such. There's the library but he always left his work in the laboratory."

"Whoever's after the papers won't know that," I said. "Take care. Always make sure you have staff in the house at night. And be sure to lock up securely each evening."

"Sure, Mike," the girl said. "We have strong shutters actually, but we never use them."

"I'd use them from now on," I said. "Just while this thing lasts."

"Sure Mike," the girl said again. "I

don't think I need worry tonight. Not with a man with a gun in the house."

She got up abruptly.

"It's about time you were in bed. You'll feel great in the morning."

"I feel a whole lot better already," I said.

I followed her out across the hall and up the spiral staircase, shrouded in shadow now. She showed me into a big room and switched on a low-powered lamp by the bed. I was so tired I hardly saw her leave the room. I heard the door slam behind her and then I was out of the dressing gown.

I hit the sack and went out like a zombie. When I woke it was moonlight. There was just enough light for me to make out the details of the room. The bedside lamp was out. I didn't remember putting it off. Something moved in the room then. I reached under the pillow for the Smith-Wesson. I was wide awake now.

Marion Hopcroft stood looking down at me. She was smiling. She was stark naked and she looked like something out of a Greek Museum. Except that she wasn't marble.

"I thought you might be lonely," she said.

"Now why would you think that?" I said.

The sheets rustled as she slipped in beside me. Her skin was burning like fire on mine.

"Just a hunch," she whispered.

White teeth nipped playfully at my ear. I had my arms round her now. All the weariness fell away from me. The girl's tongue was tentatively exploring my mouth.

"I said you'd feel great in the morning."

"I feel great now," I told her.

I rolled over in the bed, the girl's haunches cool and firm beneath my hands.

"Let's try The Zetland Method, Mike," Marion Hopcroft breathed.

"You're the client," I said. "I always do as the client says."

11

I CAME out of deep sleep and turned over on my back. Shafts of early sunlight were spilling through the blinds. I opened my eyes and focused up. The housekeeper Anna was giving me one of her brilliant grins.

"I did knock, Mr Faraday, but I guess you didn't hear."

"Sorry," I said. "I must look a wreck."

The woman smiled again.

"Not at all. Considering everything that's happened."

I looked at her but I couldn't see any guile in her face or locate any double entendres in her voice. She fussed around with the bedcover. I gave a quick look at the pillow next me. There was no sign of the girl. Even the pillow had been smoothed as clear and blank as a con man's face. She must have left in the early dawn without waking me. Just as well under the circumstances. Anna put the big tray with its tall legs down on the coverlets to straddle my body.

"Just take your time, Mr Faraday. It's not nine o'clock yet. Miss Hopcroft says she'll join you for breakfast below at ten, if you can make it all right."

"I'll make it," I said.

The housekeeper grinned again. She wore a silk blouse that hugged her breasts and a knee-length skirt. She had pretty sensational legs. She couldn't have been more than about forty now that I studied her more closely. I saw then that her hair was tinted an ash colour. I must have been half-blind the previous evening. She smiled again like she knew what I was thinking. I watched her can wiggle all the way to the door.

When that entertainment was over I focused up on the tray. There was grapefruit juice so cold there was a rime of frost on the glass. I drank the juice, ate the hot buttered toast and washed it down with the scalding hot coffee. Then I got out the bed. I wasn't wearing anything now because of the extra-curricular exercise during the night and I looked at myself critically in the long mirror.

The cuts didn't look any better but they were clean and healing nicely. I went through into the bathroom and showered and washed off the iodine stains. While I was doing that I heard the bedroom door open. I didn't take any notice and presently whoever it was went away.

I found a razor set on the bathroom shelf, probably belonging to the Professor and did a tolerable job on my face. By the time I had my shirt and underwear on I looked almost human. When I got back to the bedroom I found that Anna had brought my suit. She'd made a great job of it. I put on the pants and shoes and knotted my tie and went down without my coat.

The girl was sitting in a big glass

conservatory with tropical plants piled all around. She sat at a white circular table and watched me with sparkling green eyes. She had on the same outfit as the night before, or a similar one but there was a difference now; I knew what was underneath it and I looked at her with even more interest.

She flushed like she knew what I was thinking and glanced down at her plate. The doors of the conservatory were open and latched back and there was a fine view of green lawns and palms and the greeny-blue of the Pacific beyond. I went and sank down into a chair opposite the girl and didn't say anything for a moment.

Sprinklers were going on the grass below and a Japanese gardener, wearing a wide-brimmed hat and stripped to the waist was walking through the spray and looking like he was enjoying it.

"At the risk of being banal, good morning," I said.

Marion Hopcroft smiled.

"Did you sleep well?" she said mockingly.

The housekeeper was wheeling in with a trolley piled high with silver dishes at the moment and she looked shrewdly from me to the girl and then back again.

"Pretty well under the circumstances," I said.

The girl leaned forward and sniffed appreciatively at the dish Anna was putting down on the table. The housekeeper started ladling bacon, eggs, grilled liver and ham on to the girl's plate. Slices of grapefruit and long strips of toast followed. There was chopped grilled tomatoes and all sorts of other stuff. I was almost sitting up begging by the time she got to me.

"How are the wounds?" the girl said, pouring black coffee for the two of us. "Cream?"

I shook my head.

"Healing up just fine."

"Would you like any more, Mr Faraday?" Anna smiled.

In the clear sunlight, now that I could see her properly, she was improving by the minute.

"No thanks", I said. "I shall explode otherwise."

"Surprising how your appetite develops in the clear air up here," the housekeeper said.

I looked at her closely but there was nothing but sincerity and friendship in her face. Else she was the best actress who ever lived.

"Try some of this home-baked bread and fresh butter."

I allowed her to shovel two slices on to my side plate. "I'll ring if we want anything else," Marion Hopcroft said.

I was already getting into the biggest breakfast I'd seen outside a lumber-camp. Anna was one of the best cooks I'd come across too. Half an hour later I'd not only got through the meal but the girl was shovelling fresh strips of bacon on to my plate.

I put sugar in my third cup of coffee and looked out to where the

Pacific was coming in in long, lazy swells. A big, twelve-metre yacht with a white hull was doing some fancy manoeuvres on its way out to sea and a character in scarlet shorts and a white shirt was trying to do a handstand on the bowsprit. Leastways, that's what it looked like from this distance.

Two blondes in flesh-coloured tights that made them look naked stood and admired the skipper's work. The girls were bare-breasted and for a minute or two it made me fancy a life on the ocean wave. That is until I looked at Marion Hopcroft's smile across the table.

"I hope you enjoyed your stay, Mike," she said, with a strange, shy expression on her face.

"I'll never forget it, honey," I said.

I sat back in my chair and got out my pack of cigarettes. I found one that was less bent than the others and the girl came around the table to light it for me with a gold lighter shaped like a space capsule. I feathered out blue smoke and felt that with a little care I might make it to forty.

The girl took my hands in her own and winced at my cut palms. My ribs and the rest of my body were beginning to ache a treat now but I felt ready for the next move. Whatever that might be.

"We haven't discussed this business at all, Mike," she said.

"Nothing to discuss," I told her. "I'm still out as bait. There's bound to be another move after yesterday's failure."

"Take care, Mike," the girl said.

She came behind my chair and her lips gently brushed the back of my neck.

"Sure," I said. "And don't forget what I said about this place. Keep up those precautions until you get the word from me."

"Sure," the girl said.

She went back to her own chair. She shivered slightly.

"I shall be glad when the funeral's over."

"It's always tough," I said. "But it will pass. Would you like me to come along?"

Marion Hopcroft's green eyes were full of affection.

"I appreciate it, Mike. But you have too much to do already. I can handle it."

"Fine," I said. "You want me to have a look around among your father's effects while I'm here?"

The girl shook her head.

"You can take it from me there's nothing here. Don't ask me how I know. I just know. Father never kept anything like that at home. The Zetland Method, whatever it is, is at the Malmo Institute or maybe in his safe deposit. I haven't had time to go into that yet."

"That's it, then," I said.

I got up to get my coat. She saw me to the front door.

"Thanks for everything," I said.

The girl's smile lasted me all the way back into L.A.

★ ★ ★

Stella looked at me sardonically. This afternoon she wore an open-neck silk shirt and a short grey skirt. It was one of her little-girl outfits that always had the opposite effect on me. She came over to me and ran cool fingers along the side of my jaw. It seemed to take the whole of the pain of my body away.

"Thanks for sending the Smith-Wesson out, honey," I said.

"I figured you might need it," she said. "But now I've seen you a band-aid would have been more practical."

I grinned. Stella went and sat on her own desk and swung a shapely knee. It was late in the day and the air had that heavy, sticky feel when there's a storm in the offing. That and the smog and the gasoline fumes in the atmosphere made a unique blend so that I could tell L.A. from a hundred other atmospheres.

The new plastic fan Stella had bought

145

was circulating freely but it was only re-distributing the stale air. I had my coat off and my sleeves rolled up and I was trying to keep the palms of my hands from Stella's gaze. She gets a little motherly when I've been knocked about and I hadn't got time tonight. It might lead to other things.

Stella had just been doing a long session of note-taking and she'd stayed on a bit to type the stuff up. I lit a cigarette and feathered the smoke to the ceiling. The atmosphere was so thick the whirring of the fan blades hardly disturbed the plumes.

"You put the envelope in the bank?" I said.

Stella nodded.

"Sure," she said. "You figure it'll do any good?"

"It'll do some good," I said. "The opposition — whoever they are — have tried everything else. I figure they'll consider the kid-glove approach now that the other tactics have failed."

Stella shrugged. She slid off the desk

146

with a lithe movement.

"It's your body," she said.

I shifted in the chair, opened the drawer and tapped the Smith-Wesson harness.

"I shan't be jumped again," I said. "Leastways, not without getting a few slugs off first."

Stella went over to the alcove and switched on the coffee percolator. She put her head round the ground-glass screen.

"So you're going to sit here and stake yourself out."

"Something like that," I said. "They've tried the house and all the other dumb plays. That only leaves the office."

"So you'd like some coffee before I go," Stella said.

"Try me," I said.

Stella smiled and went back to the alcove. I sat on smoking and thinking about nothing in particular, half-listening to the clinking of cups in the background. It's one of the times of day I like best. My body was throbbing nicely now but with that good feeling which means that flesh is healing. Though I wouldn't have been in shape for gym work-outs just now. Stella came back and put the brimming cup on my blotter.

"I'll be at home if you want me," she said.

"Sure, honey," I said.

She hesitated by the desk, looking at her wristlet watch.

"If you want a second cup you'll have to pour your own."

"I've still got strength for that," I said. "Just leave the waiting-room door on the latch."

Stella grinned. She ran her hand along the side of my jaw and then skipped out. I heard her footsteps beat a rapid tattoo across the waiting-room floor. Then the outer office door clicked and I was alone with the dusk, the neons and my aching bones.

I sat there for what seemed like a long time. The fan re-distributed the exhausted air. Presently I got up and poured myself another cup before it got cold. It was in the true canon. I carried the cup back over to my desk and listened. There had been a faint sound from somewhere out in the corridor.

I opened the drawer and got out the Smith-Wesson. I pushed off the safety and laid it down on my blotter. I put a file of papers over it, so it couldn't be seen by anyone sitting in the chair in front of my desk. Then I went on stirring my coffee. I drank some more and admired the neons and the smog from my window.

It was a little cooler now. But not much. I let go the handle of the cup. I sat with my hand close to the edge of the saucer. It was about three inches from the butt of the Smith-Wesson under the folder of papers. It was a comforting feeling. There was only my desk lamp on. It cast a warm glow over the desk and the surrounding area but left my face in shadow.

I finished off my coffee and pushed

the cup away. I left my hand on the blotter where it would get to the gun-butt in a hurry. A board creaked somewhere in the waiting-room. A muscle fretted in my cheek. I must have sat there for all of half an hour. It seemed like half a year. I was still sitting in the same position, my cigarette butt smoking in the earthenware tray, when the lock on the office door snicked and somebody eased into the room.

12

I MOVED my finger fractionally nearer the butt of the gun.

"You might flip that light-switch on," I said. "You'll find it a lot easier to see me."

A dry chuckle sounded in the warm silence.

"And vice versa."

Light flooded down from the overhead fitting. I blinked a little but I didn't get up or move my position at the desk.

"Good evening, Mr Faraday," the voice went on.

It was low and cultured, a man's voice that was sure of itself.

"You must forgive my discreet method of entry."

"Some people would call it other things," I said.

The half-open door had obscured my visitor until now. He'd evidently been making sure I was alone. Now he eased round it, closed it after him and came on down the room toward me. He was a lean, dapper figure, cool in a tropical suit. He had a lean, tanned face with a well-clipped mustache.

"You must give me the address of your tailor," he said drily.

"I had an argument with some characters yesterday," I said. "I'm going on home to change later. If nothing else happens to prevent me."

My visitor threw his hands wide in a theatrical gesture.

"What's to prevent you?"

"What indeed?" I said.

I went over to the window and pulled down the slats of the blind. There was a big black sedan parked opposite our block. A man was standing leaning against it, looking up in the direction of the window.

"They wouldn't be waiting for you, I suppose?"

The lean man had come to stand beside me. He looked down and laughed. It was an agreeable sound until one came to analyse the hollowness in back of it. I went to sit at my desk. I put my hand out close to the Smith-Wesson butt and waited for him to sit down opposite me.

He had very blue eyes that looked startling in that brown face, and but for a narrow, rat-trap mouth he would have been handsome. He wore a rainbow-coloured tie that hung in a big knot under the wide points of his immaculate white shirt. There was a tiny scar at the right-hand corner of his mouth which gave him a more humorous look than he would have otherwise had. He looked to me like a character who wouldn't stand messing around with. He glanced at a gold wristlet watch on his hairy left wrist and folded his hands over his kneecap.

He rocked to and fro in his chair for a moment without saying anything but his blue eyes were stabbing at the corners of the room. I knew he'd figured out all the angles before he entered the waiting-room. His goons outside would have made sure I was alone before they let him up. The lean man smiled slowly and looked at me from under his eyelids.

"You must have an interesting line of work. It is Mr Faraday, the investigator?"

"That's what it says on the door."

"You're too modest, Mr Faraday," the lean man went on. "You've got quite a reputation around town."

"I haven't heard your name," I said.

The lean man straightened up in the chair and looked at me lazily.

"Dobbs," he said readily. "C. George Dobbs."

His eyes flickered to the dossier on my desk. He flicked it with strong, square fingers.

"And incidentally, Mr Faraday, you can put away the heater. No-one's going to hurt you."

I grinned. I shifted the dossier. I put the safety on the Smith-Wesson, slid it across the desk and put it with the harness in the drawer.

"That's nice to know," I said. "Especially coming from someone who made the entrance you did."

Dobbs' eyes flickered.

"Don't get me wrong, Mr Faraday," he said. "I have to be careful in my line of business."

"So do I," I said.

I held up the palms of my hands toward him.

"Just what is your line of business?"

Dobbs gave a low whistle. He stared at my hands for a long moment.

"I didn't say," he said. "We'll get to it."

He drew his chair closer to the desk.

"Just how did you get those hands, Mr Faraday?" He put his head on one side and studied me closely.

"And the cuts, come to that."

"I fell out the back of a truck yesterday," I said. "It was going quite a lick. I'm lucky to be here."

I swapped glances with him for a

long moment. The bright blue eyes were cool and steady.

"Your business seems to be a dangerous one," Dobbs said.

"Sometimes," I said. "Like now. I'm just trying to decide what yours is."

Dobbs put his hand up and scratched the side of his nose.

"You must excuse me, Mr Faraday. I'm taking a long time getting to the point. But then I'm from out-of-town. And I like to size people up first."

"So do I," I said.

Dobbs smiled faintly and leaned back in the chair.

"Have you come to any conclusion about me?"

I shook my head.

"Not entirely. You could be very dangerous if crossed. But you'd probably be on the square. If it suited you."

Dobbs drew in his lips and made a wry face.

"Not a bad estimate, Mr Faraday," he said mockingly. "I think you might be in a position to help me."

"That's what I'm here for," I said.

I leaned back in my chair and waited for Dobbs to go on.

"You said something about being tossed out of a truck yesterday, Mr Faraday. Would you care to elaborate?"

"Why should it interest you?" I said. "Besides, I don't talk about my cases."

Dobbs looked at me with suddenly hard eyes.

"An excellent rule, Mr Faraday. And normally I wouldn't ask you. But I have a feeling we might be talking about the same business."

★ ★ ★

The room seemed to have become very quiet and close. I stared at Dobbs for a long moment. Then I eased up in the chair.

"You'll have to spell it out, Mr Dobbs. I'm not sure I follow you."

Dobbs sat upright and eased forward across the desk until his eyes were boring into mine.

"I'll lay my cards on the table, Mr Faraday. I'm part of a big organisation. One of our functions is to keep an eye on and estimate the commercial potential of new processes in the scientific and industrial fields."

"So?" I said.

"So this," Dobbs said.

He glanced round the room quickly, like there might be someone bugging the place.

"One of the methods is through the perfectly legitimate practice of reading and evaluating technical papers and articles in the scientific and industrial journals. Some while ago we came on an interesting thesis by a scientist called Hopcroft."

Something in my face must have given me away because Dobbs smiled slowly.

"I see that rings a bell."

"You have the advantage of me," I said. "I don't know anything about any such thesis."

Dobbs raised his hand.

"Hear me," he said gently. "It was only an indication, nothing more, of lines of inquiry Hopcroft was carrying out. But to people in the field it meant a great deal more to those able to read it aright."

Dobbs eased himself in his chair.

"This talking makes one's throat dry," he said.

I grinned. I reached for the lower drawer of the desk.

"Only bourbon," I said. "No ice, if that suits."

Dobbs nodded gravely.

"It suits."

He watched me closely as I poured.

"No water," he said.

He lifted his glass in salute.

"Here's to a successful collaboration."

I lifted my glass and waited for him to go on.

"Our organisation evaluated and filed the information," Dobbs said. "One needs a lot of patience in this line of work. From hints thrown out from time to time, we learned that Hopcroft was carrying on with his research. We hoped to contact him and make an offer."

"And did you?" I said.

Dobbs gave me a sharp look.

"Not in the way you mean," he said. "Someone else got there before us. The Professor was a frightened man."

"You're talking about The Zetland Method," I said.

The effect on Dobbs was astonishing. He paused with his glass halfway to his lips. The amiable features of his face had gone. Instead, there was only the thin line of the lips and the ugly look of the eyes. It was quite a revealing moment.

"So you do know about this?" he said.

I shrugged.

"I thought you'd already checked. Sure, I know something about the set-up. I was there the night Hopcroft died. Killed by a hit-and-run. His daughter hired me to go into the background.

But you know so much you must have figured that too."

Dobbs slowly put the glass down on the desk in front of him.

"Don't get so touchy, Mr Faraday."

"You'd be touchy if you'd been sapped and snatched," I said. "I damn near killed myself getting out of that furniture truck yesterday. That's why I keep the Smith-Wesson handy."

Dobbs permitted himself a smile about six millimetres wide.

"I understand," he said.

"That's more than I do," I said. "What is The Zetland Method? And what's it worth?"

Dobbs shook his head. There was the remnants of the smile on his lips.

"No dice," he said.

I leaned back and frowned over toward the window.

"How do I know you didn't have Hopcroft killed?" I said.

"You don't," the lean man said. "But do I look stupid."

I shook my head.

"I have to give you a point there. A less stupid-looking man I've never met."

Dobbs gave a brief, genuine smile.

"I already told you we don't do business like that. We would have made Hopcroft a commercial offer."

"Why didn't you?" I said.

Dobbs spread his hands out over my desk. He looked reflectively at his glass. I leaned over and re-filled it for him.

"I'm an agent in this matter, Mr Faraday. It's not my place to make deals on my own. My principals would have moved when they felt the time ripe. Hopcroft must have licked his problems on the Method."

"How do you make that out?" I said.

Dobbs shook his head slowly.

"Easy to see this isn't your scene," he said. "What would be the point of knocking off someone like Hopcroft if they hadn't perfected a potentially valuable commercial formula? Kill him before and they kill the golden goose.

So I figure that he'd finished his work."

"You got a point," I said.

Dobbs looked at me through narrowed eyes.

"Too true I got a point, Mr Faraday. It's my guess we're dealing with amateurs."

"We?" I said.

Dobbs smiled. He was finding it more easy to do now.

"I don't think you'll turn down my proposition when you've heard it," he said. "Especially when there's ten G's in it for you. With ten more of the same on completion."

I looked at Dobbs for a moment without saying anything. He picked up his glass and took a long, slow sip.

"That's right, Mr Faraday. The Zetland method is worth a lot of money. So much, in fact, that we're willing to pay you handsomely for it."

"How do you know the characters who killed Hopcroft haven't already got it?"

Dobbs shook his head.

163

"They wouldn't still be bouncing you around. What about the daughter?"

"I'm sure she hasn't got it." I said.

Dobbs put his finger-tips together and studied them like the answers to all his questions were engraved on his nails.

"How do you know I wouldn't take The Zetland Method for myself as well as your fee?" I said.

Dobbs almost bust out laughing this time.

"Firstly, I checked your record," he said. "Secondly, you wouldn't be able to make anything out of it. It's just a sheet of paper with some figures on it."

He drained his glass and leaned forward, his eyes boring into mine.

"Thirdly, no profit. You wouldn't last long. I told you I was with a big organisation. Those boys outside, for instance. I can call on another fifty like that if I have to. I'm one of the best contract men in the country."

"I wouldn't want to mess with you," I said.

Dobbs cleared his throat.

"Take my advice, Mr Faraday, and don't do it. There's no future in it. But play ball with me and there's a good deal of money in it for you."

"I'd like some time to think about it," I said.

Dobbs got up.

"Don't take too long," he said. "I'll come back for your answer this time tomorrow night. We'll go into the details then."

"You seem pretty sure I'll take the case," I said. Dobbs put his hands in his pockets. He looked like a younger version of Clifton Webb as he stood on the other side of my desk.

"You'll take the case, Mr Faraday," he said easily. "It wouldn't be worth your while not to."

I sat there until his footsteps had died away down the corridor. Then I poured myself another drink.

13

A THIN rain was falling as I slotted the Buick into a vacant spot in the parking lot and killed the motor. I lit a cigarette and frowned through the windshield at the outlines of the Malmo Institute through the rain.

I checked my wrist-watch. I knew that quitting-time was in half an hour from what the girl had told me. I switched on the radio while I waited for my man to show. I sat there for an hour before anything happened. Anything significant, that is. Plenty of people who worked at the Institute came out, got into their automobiles and went away.

But nobody came near the white Dodge I was staking-out. The rain drummed monotonously on the windshield and I began to get the feeling

I'd had hundreds of times on such assignments. It's compounded of the sound of running drains; the smell of dampness on the upholstery; stale cigarette smoke; and a gnawing consciousness inside one that I was in the wrong profession. It's a feeling I get three or four times a year and it's hard to shake.

I'd smoked three cigarettes and was about to set fire to a fourth when my man showed; he wore a smart white belted raincoat and a snap-brim fedora that made him look like something out of a Warner Brothers forties movie. I smiled to myself. Life was at last beginning to imitate art.

I waited until I could see the white smoke of his exhaust before I started my own motor. The white Dodge cruised across the parking lot and down the ramp toward the street. I followed at a leisurely pace, making sure the other car was well ahead. The driver nudged it into the traffic, which was fairly light for the moment, and started making time toward the west. I slotted in about three cars behind and followed at a steady cruising speed.

The Dodge was easy to follow, being such a light colour, so it didn't seem as though there would be much difficulty. I wasn't quite sure what I was going to do. If Dobbs was on the level, and there was no reason to believe otherwise, there were two sets of people interested in The Zetland Method. I didn't intend to wait around any longer to make a punchbag. I was going to do some bouncing of my own.

I'd finally gotten rid of my worn-out clothing of the previous day. Tonight I wore a light tweed suit and the harness of the Smith-Wesson made a comforting pressure against my shoulder muscles as I spun the wheel, following the white car toward the beach road. My hands were healing nicely and apart from a few aches and pains now and then when I made a sudden movement, I was almost as good as new.

We were out in the open now, the Pacific sad and green behind its curtain of rain. The white Dodge was still two cars in front, doing a steady sixty so I just bored on, my mind as dull and blank as the noise given out by the windscreen wipers. The beaches were deserted except for an athletic character in shorts and a wind-cheater who was doing a solitary run beside the combers.

We passed a boardwalk pier and some closed-up beach concessions. I woke up. The Dodge had turned off at an intersection about a quarter of a mile ahead. I could see it nosing up the cliff road. I signalled and changed position into the centre lane. I knew where the car was going now. There was a place called Funland set atop the cliff. It was an ideal spot for a meeting on a sunny day but a bit conspicuous on an evening like this.

The sky was getting dark and I switched on my sidelights as I followed up the zig-zag bends, the beach and the sea spreading out behind me as I climbed. The rain still kept up and neons were beginning to prick the dusk below until the whole bay was ringed with fire. I bored on until an enormous hoop of white bulbs lit the sky ahead. Inside the hoop, red neon spelled out: FUNLAND.

★ ★ ★

I drove the Buick through two big iron gates, pinned back, and over a tarmac car-park until I found a space. The light was going rapidly from the sky now. I walked on over to the edge of the car-park. There was a rail there which protected visitors from the cliff edge. There was a lot more light down over the sea. Silhouetted against it, I could see a hang-glider.

A character in white shorts and a dark sweater, was hanging in the filigree-mesh of wires underneath broad yellow wings and soaring upwards in a thermal. Attached only by the safety harness, and manoeuvring by shifting his weight, he looked like a great butterfly against the glowing surface of the sea.

Either he'd launched himself from somewhere along the cliff or he was utilising the dunes in back of the beach; either way he was taking a hell of a risk at this time of the evening, with the freeway underneath, the cliffs in back and the sea beyond. But then he was taking a hell of a risk anyway by going up in such a flimsy thing. I set fire to a cigarette and grinned.

I narrowed my eyes against the afterglow as the birdman swooped around; I could see him now, clear-etched against the dark red glow in the sky. He lifted his hand briefly as if giving a benediction to L. A. Then he had dropped away and was skimming down toward the beach. I followed him as long as I could but then I'd lost him in the dusk near ground level.

I got back to the present and gum-shoed over toward the car-park entrance and eased into Funland. A blare of music came from the far distance and a Ferris wheel exploded in a riot of colours against the evening sky. The sickly smell of candy floss, cookies and hot fritters came strong and acrid in the warm air.

I'd seen the big man near the entrance while I was watching the manoeuvres of the hang-glider; that was one of the reasons I'd stayed back. He'd gone on into the concession a minute or two before. There was no hurry. I strolled on past a booth which was echoing to the hammering of gun-fire. A scarlet notice proclaimed: FIRE A REAL TOMMY-GUN AT YOUR FAVORITE POLICEMAN.

I wrinkled up my face. Some invocation to morality. No wonder there were so many cheap punks around. I'd have shot the booth owner first off. Except that there was a law against that. I grinned again and went on down the park.

There was a Fun House; carousels;

a mirror maze; Ghost-Train; speedway track; the works. The place was pretty crowded too, mostly with youngsters and middle-aged men. There didn't seem to be any in-between age-groups. Judging by the way the dollars were flowing in across the counters there was no inflation problem here. I stopped and admired a bloated clown-face which a blonde in a red sweater was hurling tennis balls at. Judging by her delivery she could have handled Babe Ruth.

White-raincoat was standing near the Ghost-Train. As I watched he paid his entrance money and went over to sit in a car near the front of the train. There was a man in a dark blue belted wind-cheater already sitting in the car. I stayed back. There was no point getting on the train. They had to come back out. So I stayed put.

I moved on after a while. It seemed like a long ride. When I got back round the other side of the concession, the train was gliding to a halt. The man in the dark wind-cheater was getting off. He had his back to me so I couldn't see his face. He went over to the guy in the booth and put some money down. He jerked a thumb back over his shoulder. White-raincoat was staying on. It seemed a screwy arrangement to me.

I hesitated whether to follow the second man or stick with white-raincoat. While I was thinking about it the second man disappeared in the crowd. I shrugged and moved on a little, fetching up in a position where I could see the Ghost-Train exit. Judging by the shrieks and laughter coming from inside it was a pretty good ride. I frowned, watching the blonde in the red sweater pass. The two men had a smart method of exchanging information. I wished I'd gotten aboard the train now. In the dark I might have learned something. The important part of the evening was over and I wasn't any the wiser.

I could feel the reassuring bulk of

the Smith-Wesson against the webbing harness. But the new suit was a little tight around the shoulders. It had shrunk or I'd grown. Either way it made it difficult for me to get at the butt of the revolver.

I ducked behind a booth and transferred it to my raincoat pocket. When I got back in front of the Ghost-Train concession the chain of cars had just rocked to a halt. White-raincoat sat on immobile while the cars around him emptied and re-filled. I stared. There was something badly wrong. I got over to the glassed-in booth and planked my money down. I got into a car a couple behind white-raincoat just as the thing started to move. We lurched on down through the door-flap into pitch darkness.

Something brushed my face with icy fingers. I had the Smith-Wesson out now. People were screaming all around me as the train lurched on through the darkness. I could see the big man's figure silhouetted against a luminous green spider's web that we were headed for. He hadn't changed position. The cars lurched again and I got outside, clinging on the safety rail. I put my foot on the linkage between the cars and got into the next. I was only one behind the big guy now. He didn't seem to notice anything.

Skeletons were zooming at us from all angles accompanied by deafening electronic effects. The screams were even more vivid than the electronics. I made up my mind then. The cars plunged into darkness. We were climbing rapidly uphill. I got on to the linkage joining the cars and vaulted over into the seat next to white-raincoat without being thrown off. The cars were thundering downhill at a frenetic speed. I had the gun in my right hand, clasped the rail with my left. I had to shout to make myself heard.

"Do we talk now or are you going to ride all night?"

There was enough light now for me to see white-raincoat's expression.

He didn't answer. A banshee wailing filled all the dark tunnel, seemed to split my head. The big man sagged against me.

Green lightning writhed across his features. His lips were blue, the blackened tongue protruding. I knew Mackensen was dead long before I saw the wire loop round his neck, buried in the folds of discoloured flesh.

14

I LET go the corpse of the Malmo Institute Director like a scalded cat. The howling went on, filling the whole tunnel. A green skeleton on a green horse was galloping balefully alongside the rocking cars now. Highly appropriate. I got the hell out quick and worked my way back to my original car. I was sitting there blinking when the Ghost-Train battered its way out through the doors and into the garish neon-lit sky-line of Funland. It had been some ride. I slid the Smith-Wesson back into the harness as we emerged and hit the ground before the cars stopped moving. I was a hundred yards away and out of sight as the passengers started getting off. I hot-footed it back to the car-park and got the Buick. Another great lead gone. The man in the wind-cheater would be ten miles away by now. I wondered if he knew anything about furniture removals.

I looked at my watch. I had an hour and a half before Dobbs was due at my office. I eased the Buick out gently through the entrance gates. I started making time down the bluff and back in to L.A. No-one followed me.

It was raining again now and I got the wipers going. I made a steady pace along the shore-road, thinking up my story and trying to make some sense of what was happening.

It wasn't any good so I gave it up. I found a place to park near our building and got outside a coffee and a sandwich. The elevator wasn't working this time of the evening so I walked on up to our floor. There were still lights coming from the inner office so I guessed Stella hadn't knocked off yet. Nevertheless I broke out the Smith-Wesson and eased my way quietly through the waiting room.

Stella was sitting at her machine. She

smiled as I came through the door.

"It's already brewing," she said.

"I could use it," I told her.

I went over to my desk and sat down and frowned at the blotter. Stella put her head on one side and regarded me in silence for a moment.

"Trouble?"

I nodded.

"We just lost the head man at the Malmo Institute."

Stella's eyes were wide. She reached for her scratch-pad as I went on talking.

"He took a one-way ticket on a fun fair railway," I said.

I reached for my pack of cigarettes. I lit up and blew blue smoke at the ceiling. Stella got up and went over to the alcove. She came back and put the coffee down on the desk in front of me. She came back with her own cup and the sugar.

"Biscuits in the tin," she said. "I forgot to tell you. Dobbs rang in. He said he might be a little late."

I nodded. I stirred the coffee and tasted it. It was just right. I went on talking, gave Stella the story of what had happened at Funland. She took it all down. I was on my second cup before we finished. Stella sat looking at me, her chin on her hands.

"It puts Mackensen in the clear,". she said.

"That'll no doubt be a big consolation to him," I said.

Stella smiled.

"What do you intend to do now? Wait until the Malmo people knock each other off?"

"That would be one way of breaking the case," I said. "Elimination."

Stella smiled again. More faintly this time.

"It might be Dobbs' crowd," she said.

I shook my head.

"Unlikely. From what I saw of him he was a highly disciplined character. He wants me to get The Zetland Method for him. That's the act of a

181

reasoning man. My guess is he could be pretty violent. He's got the organisation for it. But only as a last resort."

"You better watch your step, Mike," Stella said.

"You seem to be losing all confidence in me since I fell off the back of a truck," I said.

"It may have addled your brains," Stella said darkly.

She stopped. There were heavy footsteps coming down the corridor. The waiting room door opened. I went out. A gigantic man with a face of hammered bronze was standing there. He must have been all of seven feet tall. His ears stuck out like jug-handles; he had fists like hams; and there was a dent in his forehead like a sledge-hammer had tried to crack it. The way he was built the sledge-hammer probably got the worst of it. Otherwise he looked pretty amiable.

He wore a belted blue raincoat and his blond hair was clipped pretty close all over his scalp. He had deep brown eyes and there was a good-humoured look on his battered face. I put him down as an ex-pug now employed as professional bodyguard. His voice was low and soft when he spoke; surprising for such a big man.

"Mr Faraday? Mr Dobbs sent me to pick you up."

"I thought he was coming here," I said.

The big man shook his head.

"I'm Sprowle. Mr Dobbs' associate. He'd like you to come with me."

Stella opened the door and stood blinking at the man-mountain. The big pug preened himself; a smile cracked up his features.

"I'm Sprowle. Pleased to meet you, lady."

"Likewise," Stella said.

She looked at me dubiously.

"I'm just going for a little ride with this gentleman," I told Stella. "I'd like to know where."

The big pug shifted his feet.

"I'm not supposed to say. We're in

a motel on the edge of town at the moment."

He smiled again at Stella.

"It's all right, lady. No harm will come to Mr Faraday."

"You bet," I said. "But we go in my car."

The pug gave Stella a half-bow and looked at me gravely.

"That will be perfectly satisfactory, Mr Faraday."

I turned back to Stella.

"You'd better phone the girl. Tell her I'm working on things."

"Sure, Mike," Stella said. "You'll ring in tonight?"

"Just as soon as I get back," I said.

★ ★ ★

We took my car. The big pug sat in the passenger seat and blinked dimly at the dashboard. It didn't make him look any more intellectual.

"I didn't want to say nothing in front of the lady, Mr Faraday," he said in a voice like two sheets of sandpaper being rubbed together. "But no messing around, eh?"

"I don't mess around with people your size," I told him. "Especially when there's a big sedan with two more gentlemen travelling in rear of us."

Sprowle nodded like my answer satisfied him. I looked at him inquiringly.

"Just keep going straight, Mr Faraday. I'll tell you when to turn off."

The traffic was fairly light this time of the evening and we didn't have a lot of trouble getting across town. He nodded when we got to the beach road and I turned off, the tyres shirring as I straightened up. We were running alongside the ocean now so I opened up a little. The big black sedan pulled up to within twenty yards and kept pace behind.

"You like your work?" I said.

The big man was lighting a cigarette. He half-turned toward me, the glare of the match making a great hollow of blackness in the dent of his forehead. I

185

couldn't see the expression in his eyes. "Don't you?"

The gentleness was back in his voice again now. He'd evidently laid aside the mask of the heavy.

"Sure," I said. "But it's a little different."

Sprowle shook his massive head.

"I don't see why. We're both soldiers, ain't we? We both take orders. Me from Mr Dobbs at the moment. You from whatever client hires you."

I looked at him with more respect.

"That's one way of putting it."

The big guy shrugged.

"It's the only way to put it," he said.

It was a flat statement, not to be contradicted. I didn't try.

"Known Dobbs long?" I said.

Sprowle shook his head. His ears looked more like jug handles than ever.

"I don't talk about my employers, Mr Faraday. I wouldn't expect you to talk about your clients. A man's got to have respect."

"You put a lot of store on loyalty don't you?"

Sprowle nodded violently. The sparks from his cigarette tip made a dancing chain of light within the car.

"Too damned true I do. That's all there is, ain't it?"

I looked at him again. I was beginning to like the big man. I was sure now that he'd had nothing to do with the furniture van job.

"You got a first name?" I said.

The big man's face was in darkness.

"They got a lot of comic names for me," he said. "My real friends call me Chick."

I turned again at the next intersection off the beach as Sprowle put a big hand on my shoulder.

"What do I call you?" I said.

Sprowle screwed up his eyes like the smoke was hurting him.

"Well now, that's a big question, Mike," he said. "It depends on your attitude, really."

"We'll get along fine, Chick," I said.

Sprowle grinned. Then he took the cigarette out of his mouth and chuckled to himself in the darkness of the car like I'd made a great joke. We were climbing up a small plateau to where red and green neon spelt out the name of the Pinewood Motel; the cars on the beach road below passed like chains of fireflies in the night. The sea looked green and phosphorescent farther out.

"Earth hath not anything to show more fair," Sprowle chanted.

I looked at him. I guess my jaw must have dropped a few millimetres because he gave a throaty chuckle. The dent in his forehead was a big pool of shadow as he turned toward me.

"Wentworth," he said.

"Really," I told him.

I fought the Buick in through a wrought iron archway and followed the curving drive of the motel around.

"He was an English poet guy," he said.

"Wordsworth," I said.

Sprowle looked at me blank-faced.

"Thats what I said. Wentworth. So you got culture too?"

I didn't bother to answer that. Sprowle pointed down the driveway with a vast thumb and I kept on going, the Buick's tyres crunching over the gravel.

"Number 56," he said.

The numbers were on white-painted boards set at intervals at the side of the path, odds on the left, evens on the right. I followed them down in the light of the headlamps. I stopped the car and killed the motor. Silence crowded in, except for the shrilling of grasshoppers. I saw in the rear-mirror the black sedan pull in behind us. The headlights winked out. Sprowle got out his side of the car and waited for me. I got the keys and slammed the door behind me.

There was a big Mercedes standing in the driveway of No 56. There were lights on in the cabin. I fell in abreast of Sprowle and we walked on up the cement path toward the front door. It opened before we got to it. A short, bearded man stood in the opening and waited for us to come. The two big men in dark suits stood at the end of the cement path. They obviously weren't coming in. Equally obviously they were the heavies Dobbs had had waiting for him outside my place the day before.

The bearded man nodded affably as I got inside the door.

"Mr Faraday."

He stood aside to let me pass. The big man came in behind me. Sprowle had to duck to get under the lintel, he was so gigantic. We were in a small hallway with pine-panelled walls and an ivory-coloured telephone on a teak stand. The bearded man was bolting the door behind us.

Sprowle stayed in back of me while the man with the beard opened a door immediately in front of us. The light was brighter in here and I blinked. There was a ceiling light and two shaded lamps burning. The walls were pine-panelled like a Tyrolean chalet and there were antlers over the stone fireplace which had imitation logs in the grate. A radio was burbling soothing music low down and the heavy curtains were drawn across the windows.

A striking-looking dark girl was sitting on a leather divan. She had long, insolent-looking legs and a body to go with them. She was smoking a cigarette through a green jade holder and wore an expression like she thought Faye Dunaway was old hat. I liked her cut.

Dobbs was sitting at a low table opposite the girl and studying some pencilled notes in front of him. He got up as we came in and came down the room to meet us. Sprowle went over and switched off the radio.

Dobbs wore a lightweight grey suit this evening and a conservative charcoal colour tie to go with it. He looked cool and dapper. The small scar at the side of his mouth twitched as he opened his mouth to smile. He gave me a hard, dry hand to shake.

"It was good of you to join us, Mr Faraday," he said.

15

"DID I have much choice?"
I said.

The dark girl on the divan smiled. Dobbs looked amused.

"Frankly, no," he said.

He motioned to the bearded man who went over to a buffet that was loaded with bottles.

"What's your answer, Mr Faraday?"

It seemed to have grown very quiet in the room. The dark girl tapped ash off her cigarette on to the carpet. Sprowle stood against the wall with his arms folded.

"I decided to join the club," I said.

Dobbs' expression didn't change but he made a subtle movement of his shoulders which said more than if he'd written me a postcard.

"You made a wise and excellent

decision," he said softly. He rubbed his hands.

"We'll celebrate with a drink and then get down to business. But first I'd like you to meet a great friend of mine. Joan, this is Mike Faraday."

He led me over to the divan.

"Mike, Joan Hart."

The girl nodded coolly but said nothing. I followed Dobbs back to the table and sat down in a low chair where I could see Dobbs and the girl. The bearded man came back to me and put down the glass of bourbon with ice at my elbow.

"How did you know?" I said.

He grinned.

"I can tell a bourbon man a mile off. You're a bourbon man."

Dobbs lifted his own glass in silent salute as we drank. The stuff wasn't half bad. Dobbs looked at me shrewdly.

"Have you seen the late edition?"

He tapped the newspaper on the table in front of him. I shook my head. He passed the Examiner over. He'd ringed a small stick of type in the stop-press. It reported the Mackensen Ghost Train kill. I looked at my watch.

"Pretty fast going," I said. "It only happened three hours ago."

I gave Dobbs a long, hard look.

"You don't miss much."

Dobbs shrugged. He swilled his glass around and looked dreamily into the bottom of it.

"Cedric here picked it up. We naturally keep tabs on the Malmo Institute. They seem to have a high mortality rate."

"So I noticed," I said. "I was there."

Dobbs stiffened. The girl took the cigarette holder out of her mouth and straightened up on the divan. The bearded man turned around from mixing his own drink and stared at me. Sprowle gave me a battered smile.

"Interesting," Dobbs said. "You didn't kill him by any chance?" I shook my head.

"Hardly. It isn't my style. How do I

know it wasn't one of your soldiers."

Dobbs' voice was level and icy.

"You got my word for it."

I shrugged.

"I won't argue with that. Especially as the odds are four to one."

Dobbs gave me a sharp glance.

"A sensible man."

"I was staking Mackensen's place out," I said. "I'd set up a little bait for the top men of the Institute. So I naturally started with the Director."

"Naturally," Dobbs said. "What was the bait?"

"That's restricted information for the moment," I said. "Anyway, I tailed Mackensen when he left his place. He went up on the bluff to Funland. He was obviously meeting someone by arrangement. He got on the Ghost Train. I hung around."

I paused and took another sip at my drink. The girl stared unblinkingly at me through her cigarette smoke.

"Another character was on the train," I said. "I only saw his back. He was a tall man in a blue wind-cheater."

"Not very helpful," Cedric said.

Dobbs made an impatient movement. He was sitting in a tensed-up position. With his thin build and lean figure he reminded me of a cat about to spring. A wild cat, of course. Not the domestic variety.

"The guy on the Ghost Train with Mackensen," I said. "He got off after the first trip. Mackensen stayed on. When he went around a third time I joined him. I found someone had put a wire trace around his neck."

There was a faint flicker of amusement round Dobbs' rat-trap mouth.

"That must have been a very distressing experience," he said.

"It was," I told him. "Especially for Mackensen."

The bearded man sniggered and Sprowle's smile opened out another millimetre. I took another sip at my drink. The evening was looking distinctly more promising.

"How do you read this, Mr Faraday?" Dobbs said.

"I don't at the moment," I said. "The girl engages me to find out who killed her father. She knew he was worried over something called The Zetland Method. It seemed logical to start with the Institute. We went through the old boy's desk before the scientific big wheels got there. We didn't find anything."

Dobbs had a very alert expression on his face now. He sat up in his chair at the other side of the table from me and cupped a lean knee in his hands. His eyes thoughtfully searched my face.

"That was a smart move. So then?"

"I had an idea," I said. "I decided to lay out some bait. I put a worthless set of figures in an envelope and wrote The Zetland Method on it. When the three principals turned up I made sure they saw it."

Dobbs' eyes were very bright. He was smiling. I knew I'd done the right thing. If he had a big organisation it would be easy enough to find out details. I'd decided to level with him. That way he'd know I was straight. And I might be able to use him to uncover The Zetland Method and the Professor's killer for me.

"Very nice," Dobbs said softly.

He looked around the room. The girl had a contented expression on her face. The bearded man stood against the wall and looked thoughtfully into his own glass.

"I set myself up," I said. "I figured that if one of his colleagues had knocked over the Professor for the formula, they'd come after me".

"And did they?" the girl said quietly.

It was the first time she'd spoken. She had a low, sensuous voice that curled the toes in one's socks.

Dobbs chuckled.

"I'll say they did," he told the girl. "Mr Faraday here got topped and had to bale out of a speeding furniture truck to escape. Enterprising. I like that."

He picked up his glass again and

stared into its contents.

"I'm glad you levelled, Mr Faraday. We have ways of checking. It would have been a bad start to our association."

I didn't say anything. After a moment Dobbs got up and went over to the other side of the room. There was a thick briefcase lying on one end of the buffet. He opened it out and I heard the crackling of paper. He came back to the table and put the thick bundle of new, unused notes in front of me. They still had the denomination bands on them.

"There you are, Mr Faraday. Ten G's I think we agreed."

"I haven't done anything yet," I said.

"You levelled," Dobbs said. "That puts you ten points ahead in my business."

I shrugged. I leaned forward and peeled off some notes. I counted them. Dobbs had gone around the other side of the table. I pushed the rest of the sheaf back.

"I'll take a thousand as a retainer. I don't know whether I can deliver yet."

"You'll deliver," Dobbs said unemotionally. "Where's the envelope with the formula now?"

"In a bank deposit," I said.

I smiled, trading glances with Dobbs.

"How do we know it's not the real formula?" he said.

"You don't," I said. "But you'd have ways of finding out."

Dobbs nodded.

"All right, Mr Faraday. A thousand for starters. The balance on delivery. "What's the next move?"

"One down and two to go," I said. "I keep on working through the Malmo Institute people. That's all we've got to go on."

There was a short silence.

"Somebody wants the stuff pretty badly," I said. "They went over my place as well."

Dobbs raised his eyebrows.

"Looks like I won't be needing my

people with you around."

"Why don't you just tackle it straight and save yourself twenty thousand?" I said.

Dobbs shook his head.

"That's something that people like you never learn, Mr Faraday. The money is peanuts. It doesn't matter. What we're after is something infinitely more valuable. But it is only of value to people who know how to use it. We've got to go carefully. The people behind us don't expose themselves. Why should they when they can employ us? In turn, we use tact ourselves. So far as the world is concerned I've never been in L.A. It's worth twenty grand to us for you to do the front work. But you have to do it right."

I sat finishing off my drink looking from Dobbs to the insolent legs of the girl and from her to Sprowle and Cedric. I put the glass back down on the table.

"It's the gritty end," I said.

Dobbs smiled again.

"Naturally. That's what we're paying you for."

I looked at the girl. She went on smoking her cigarette with that snooty look like there was a bad smell in the room. But I could tell she was interested all right. I took another sip of my drink.

"Where does Miss Hart come in?" I said.

Dobbs narrowed his eyes and looked at me. But his voice was mild enough as he replied.

"Like I said, she's just a friend."

"I guess the lady can speak for herself," I said.

Sprowle shifted his position against the wall and Cedric stopped stroking his beard like his spring has suddenly broken. The girl on the divan smiled.

"It's a fair question, Mr Dobbs. I don't mind answering it."

Dobbs shrugged.

"Right enough. It was just that I thought . . . "

"It's all right, Mr Dobbs," the girl

said calmly. "And now, if you'd just step into the other room I'd like to speak to Mr Faraday in private."

The atmosphere in the room had changed again. It was the girl who was in charge now. Dobbs got up from his chair and picked up his sheaf of papers.

"I don't get this," I said. "I thought you were heading up the operation."

Dobbs shrugged.

"You're privileged, Mr Faraday. Like I said, I'm part of a big organisation. Mrs Hart is their representative. She's come on down here to look you over."

"That important?"

The girl nodded, looking from me to Dobbs. The other two had already left the room.

"That important, Mr Faraday. That's why I wanted to see you for myself."

I grinned.

"You're seeing me, Mrs Hart."

16

DOBBS had gone out the side door. We were alone. I looked at the woman sprawled on the divan.

"You must carry some weight," I said. "Friend Dobbs doesn't seem like an easy man to handle."

The girl smiled again.

"I do to the first. He isn't to the second. But we understand one another. The organisation is too big to buck, Mr Faraday."

I went over and sat down again.

"Who's trying?" I said.

I looked at the girl for a long moment.

"Where's Mr Hart?" I said.

The girl shifted into a more comfortable position on the divan.

"He got himself killed," she said.

"I'm sorry," I told her.

She looked at me levelly.

"Don't be. It was a long time ago."

There was an awkward silence. The girl's cigarette smoke went slowly up to the ceiling. She had a broad forehead, high cheekbones that made me think of a Scandinavian; and strong, white teeth. Her lips were full and sensual, the brown eyes shrewd and cool. Now that I had time to study her fully I saw that she had a red ribbon tying back her hair which was so black as to be almost blue in sheen.

Her legs were long and sensational like I said. I could see a lot of them. She was curled up on the divan, presenting her knees toward me. Her skirt, which was dark and of medium length, was pulled up on to her thighs. She looked at me thoughtfully.

She was about thirty-two I would have said. Just the right age. Her hands were small and pink, the nails carefully trimmed and with transparent varnish. The fingers were long and slim. They were capable hands and as I looked from her legs to her face and then back again I wondered how she'd gotten into such a rough business.

She must have guessed my thoughts for she gave a faint, secret smile and blew out smoke toward the ceiling. She leaned forward to the table in front of her and took the cigarette out of the long holder. She stubbed it out in a bowl and put the holder in a small red leather handbag on the divan beside her. I noticed then she still had a wedding ring on her left hand. Next to it was a diamond cluster ring, probably her original engagement ring.

She shifted over and patted the divan next her. Her brown eyes had a strange, smoky expression. I wondered if she used drugs.

"Come and sit next to me, Mr Faraday."

"It would be a pleasure," I said. "The name's Mike."

I got up and carried my empty glass over to the sideboard. I made myself another drink and carried it back and set it down on the table near her.

"Would you like another?"

She shook her head.

"One is enough. And we've some serious talking to do."

I went and sat down near her on the divan. There was a faint, elusive perfume she was using. It was pretty powerful stuff. Or rather its effect. The perfume was subtle but it did the job it was intended for. Normally I don't go for that. But this was different.

"What do you want to know?" I said. "My track record?"

The girl shook her head again.

"We've gone into all that. What I'd like to know is your frank opinion of this case. I don't mean the girl and her father. That's nothing to do with us. We're a purely commercial organisation. And it's results that count."

"So Mr Dobbs told me," I said.

I leaned back on the divan and studied my toecaps.

"I'm waiting, Mr Faraday," the girl said calmly.

"I could come up with a fancy yarn, I said. "But that's not my style. Frankly, I don't know."

Joan Hart leaned forward stiffly and drew in her breath. She sat immobile, watching me with very bright eyes.

"What do you mean you don't know?"

Her voice cracked like a whip in the quiet room. I grinned.

"If this formula's around, I'll find it. But what if somebody blew it?"

The girl shifted along the divan until she was quite close to me. Her eyes bored into mine.

"I don't quite understand, Mr Faraday."

"Neither do I, Mrs Hart," I said. "But let's slice it this way. Professor Hopcroft's working on something called The Zetland Method. It's a valuable formula. He publishes something about it and later comes to realise that perhaps he's been indiscreet. Various people approach him to sell. That doesn't suit him."

I leaned forward and picked up my glass. All this talking was making me dry.

"Do go on," the Hart girl said.

"Colleagues at the Malmo Institute realise the commercial possibilities. They pressure him. The old boy doesn't like being pressured. But he realises he's in a hard, realistic world. A world in which people like him haven't a chance. He's even more indiscreet."

The Hart girl moved even closer to me.

"How indiscreet?"

"He lets drop that his research is complete. The Method is finished. And it works."

I leaned forward and put my glass down on the table.

"Mr Dobbs said we were dealing with amateurs. So someone runs Hopcroft down, figuring they can get the formula for nothing."

The girl was leaning forward, hanging

on my every word. I was beginning to enjoy myself now.

"Even the most complex formulae can sometimes be reduced to a couple of lines of equations. Something that a savant like Hopcroft could keep in his head."

The Hart woman drew in her breath with a sudden implosive sound. Her breasts were rising and falling like she was agitated.

"Are you suggesting, Mr Faraday, that he committed it to memory, that it doesn't exist on paper?"

"It's a possibility," I said. "We have to be prepared for failure."

"Failure isn't in my dictionary," the girl said fiercely.

I shrugged.

"Unless you've got some method of reviving the dead I don't see what we can do. Or maybe you're good with the ouija board."

The girl's eyes were stony.

"Don't make jokes, Mr Faraday."

"I'm not joking," I said. "We've got

to face up to all the possibilities. I didn't say the Method doesn't exist on paper. But what I've suggested is possible."

There was a long silence in the room.

"What about Mackensen?" the girl said at last.

"Thieves fall out," I said. "It's hardly likely the Head of the Institute would meet someone on a Ghost Train at a place like Funland if something legitimate were involved. He didn't want to be seen. That means he was up to something in my book."

The girl smiled faintly.

"You have an answer to everything in that book of yours."

I shook my head.

"I've got a lot of questions but no answers at the moment. What worries me most is the Mackensen angle. For example, was he alone of the Malmo Institute staff to be interested in the formula? If he was, who knocked him off? With your group that means there's three parties interested. Two's too many."

I sighed. I looked at Mrs Hart critically.

"I'm just an ordinary human being, Mrs Hart. Sometimes I guess right. More often than not I get beat up and tossed in the ash-can. Are you sure a classy outfit like yours wants to be associated with someone like me? I'm way out of my league."

The girl drew back a little and looked at me sharply.

"Sarcasm doesn't become you, Mr Faraday. You know you're too damn proud. And you aren't impressed by Dobbs or me for that matter. You think we're just a cheap gang of crooks steam-rollering our way across anything that gets in our path."

I shrugged. I sat back, watching the girl's face. It wasn't a difficult thing to do at any time.

"What the hell do you care what I think, Mrs Hart? I'm no-one. The only thing I've got left is a smattering of ethics. And they don't pay the rent."

"What are you doing mixed up with us then?" the girl said calmly.

"A good question," I told her.

I leaned back and got out my package of cigarettes. I offered one to the girl. She shook her head. She kept her eyes on my face. I lit up and feathered smoke at the ceiling. I looked at the door through which Dobbs and his friends had gone. It was very quiet in the place now.

"I'm still waiting, Mr Faraday," the girl said.

"I'm realistic too," I said. "Something too big to buck I go along with it."

"Or go around it," the girl said.

I nodded. I liked the Hart woman a lot, was beginning to like her more by the minute.

"Are you satisfied with me or does the inquisition go on?" I said.

"I'll let you know," the girl said.

There was a strange smile on her

face I didn't understand.

"Afterward," she said.

"Afterward?" I said.

"After we take our clothes off," Mrs Hart said.

She leaned forward and kissed me fiercely. When I came out of the coma I stubbed my cigarette out and took another nibble at my drink.

"I never argue with my employer," I said.

★ ★ ★

I looked toward the door.

"Before we get too involved, what about Dobbs?"

"He has his instructions," the girl said calmly. "That door locks from the inside. The others won't be back for three hours."

"Pretty sure of yourself weren't you?" I said.

The girl gave a little throaty chuckle.

"I always get what I want, Mr Faraday."

215

"You may be right this time," I said. "But only because it coincides with what I want."

The Hart number smiled a lazy, insolent smile.

"I'd still like to know about Dobbs," I said.

The girl shook her head. She was still sitting on the divan close to me.

"I hardly know the man."

"You're sure he isn't your husband?" I said.

There was a heavy silence in the room.

"You're going to have to explain yourself, Mr Faraday."

I shrugged.

"Some women get their kicks that way," I said.

The girl swung at me suddenly. I saw it coming. The slap of her hand made a fierce cracking sound against my forearm and I could feel the sting all the way down my arm. If the blow had landed as she intended it would have half-taken my head off.

Then I had my mouth clamped on hers and we were rolling over on the divan.

She fought silently but I knew all the moves. She whimpered as I put an arm-lock on. I only tightened up the pressure until it hurt a little. Even so she was pretty strong. I had all my work cut out to hold her down.

"You're a real bastard, Faraday," she panted.

"So I've been told," I said.

She swung at me again. This time I was ready for her and caught the blow on my shoulder. I slapped her hard against the cheek and flung her back on the cushions. Then I had her pinned by the breasts and knees. Her tongue bored into my mouth as we kissed.

"You're going to get yourself screwed if you go on like this," I said.

She forced a smile, white teeth showing against the full lips.

"That was the general idea," she said.

I let go her arms as she wriggled round. I unzipped the dress at the back. The front of it sagged forward, exposing creamy shoulders. I was bruising her lips under mine. Her kisses were salty, provocative. Her tongue never stopped working.

"I like them rough, Mr Faraday," she breathed.

"I like them all kinds, Mrs Hart," I said politely. "Just state your preference and I'll fill the order."

She grinned and tried to hit me again but I had her arms pinned.

"You'd better take that dress off or I'll rip it off," I told her.

She arched her arms up over her head and stood up on the divan. I got hold of the skirt and pulled it over her head. She had a great figure, taut and tanned, with a deep navel and everthing else to go with it. She had on minuscule white underwear, silk stockings and a suspender belt.

"The snood will be coming back in soon," I said.

Mrs Hart grinned.

"Don't tell me you don't like it?"

"I like," I said.

I pulled her bra off. Her breasts were pert and boyish.

"My boobs are too small," she giggled.

"They look all right to me," I said.

She was kneeling now, doing things with her hands. Her pants slid down easily over her thighs. It must have looked a pretty wild scene if Dobbs or any of his boys had looked in. I hoped they wouldn't. Leastways, not for a couple of hours or so.

"What worries me is what sort of report you're going to give me," I said.

Joan Hart giggled.

"Call me Joanie," she said.

"I don't think I could do that," I said. "It's rather too intimate for such a short acquaintance."

She swung at me again but I rolled her over. She arched her back.

"Satisfactory?" I said.

"I'll tell you when it's over," she breathed.

"I always try and give satisfaction," I said.

I put her firmly on her back.

17

I FELT a wreck. My joints had started aching again. Still, it had been pleasurable therapy. I drove back in to L.A., thinking over the events of the evening. Dobbs and the other two hadn't showed. Neither had anybody followed me out. It was a pretty extraordinary set-up. And Mrs Hart was the kookiest of the lot.

But if she wanted to get her kicks by indulging in such amusements I didn't mind playing along. Like I said she was the customer. And the customer was always right. She was a pretty high-powered character. Both in Dobbs' set-up if he'd been speaking the truth. And as a woman.

I turned back on to the beach-road and slotted into the traffic, watching the ribbon of fire making changing patterns on the surface of the sea to my left. I gave it up in the end. I glanced at my watch in the light from the dash-board. There was just time to pay one more call before I hit the sack.

I pulled the Buick over into the first forecourt I saw. It belonged to a diner. I went in and bought a pack of cigarettes, ordered a coffee and took it over to a table near a pay-phone. There weren't many people in this time of the evening. I put the coffee down on a shelf under the telephone and dialled Stella's number. She answered almost at once so I guessed she'd been standing by.

"Still in one piece," I said.

Stella smiled. Don't ask me how I knew. I could sense it all the way from where she was speaking. She stopped smiling at last and started talking.

"What did you find out?"

"Precious little," I said. "But that's about par for the case so far."

Stella gave a dry chuckle this time. She waited for me to go on.

"I saw Dobbs and arranged to take the assignment," I said. "He seemed satisfied."

"Did you get any money?" Stella said.

"That's genuine enough," I told her. "He wanted to give me ten thousand berries as a retainer."

"The Zetland Method must be worth something, Mike," Stella said.

"It must be a private gold-mine," I said. "I settled for a thousand in the end. That way, if I fail they may not come around to collect. But ten thousand, they'd look back for. And I might not come too well out of it."

"At least we eat," Stella said.

"In addition to Sprowle there was a bearded man there called Cedric," I said.

"You're digging up some pretty important information," Stella said.

I let that one go.

"I hope you're taking notes," I said.

"Sure," Stella said. "Make sure you post the thousand dollars on in case someone tops you before you hit town."

I grinned. I took a sip of my coffee and looked thoughtfully across the tables of the diner toward the door and the car-park beyond the windows. I couldn't see anyone hanging around outside. I'd been pretty careful and I was sure I hadn't been followed.

"There's a woman in it too," I said.

"There always is," Stella said darkly.

"A Mrs Joan Hart," I said. "Probably a phoney name. She's a big wheel the syndicate sent down to see Dobbs was spending their money wisely."

"And they still let you walk out with a thousand?"

"It's my honest face," I said. "Anyway she seemed satisfied when I left her."

It was Stella's turn to be silent.

"The Hopcroft girl phoned in just after you left," she said at last.

"Anything important?" I said.

"She just wanted to know how you were making out," she said. "Her father's funeral was this afternoon."

"Christ," I said. "I clean forgot."

"I took care of it," Stella said. "I sent some flowers for us both. The girl wanted to thank you."

"Thanks, honey," I said.

"That's what you pay me for," Stella said. "What are you doing now?"

"No sense wasting time," I told her. "I'm going up to see this Dr Eltz. He's the Assistant Director of the Malmo. He might know something."

"Good job there are only three of them," Stella said. "It might take years otherwise."

I ignored that.

"See you tomorrow," I said.

I rang off and nuzzled into my coffee. I went back to the counter of the dinette and ordered another cup and a sandwich to go with it. I ate the sandwich at a table that overlooked the car-park. The cogs in my brain were going around nicely but they weren't coming up with anything that made any sense. I watched people coming and going at nearby tables without anything really registering. It had been quite a day so far and it was only eleven p.m. now.

The bulk of the Smith-Wesson in the shoulder-holster pressed against my chest muscles as I turned to watch a blonde number walk away down the room and out to her car. I caught sight of myself in a long mirror screwed to the far wall. The suit I was breaking in almost looked as if it fitted me. I looked at the palms of my hands. They were healing nicely. I'd soon be around ninety-seven per cent fit.

I drank the last of the coffee and got up. There didn't seem any point in hanging around so I got the Buick and started making time across town.

★ ★ ★

Dr Eltz's place was a cubistic villa built like a white brick box on a quiet road near Laurel Drive. It had black glass in the windows and would have looked trendy around 1936. Now it just looked like 1936. Which was quite a way out of date. Some of the stucco ornamentation had peeled away and hair-cracks showed in the paintwork.

I tooled the Buick into a red-gravel drive that led up to the place and killed the motor. There were the obligatory shaved lawns and flowering trees to go with them. There were rough-stone cobble paths and a miniature waterfall that fell foaming over artificial rocks into an ornamental pool.

There was a dark sedan parked at the bottom of a flight of steps and diffused lights burnt atop of tall steel poles that were painted pale blue. It looked like something out of an architectural review. I got out the Buick and went over to the dark sedan. I felt the engine grille. It was still warm. Looked like Dr Eltz was at home.

I walked on up the steps to a big porch that had red and white tiles and hand-made oak benches set into recesses either side the front door.

That was a big oak affair with phoney iron handles and fancy hinges. It was standing wide open and I went on in over another tiled concourse to where a second door of frosted glass stood ajar. I frowned and stood looking at the half-open door and the buzzer.

In the end I pushed open the door and went on into a dim hallway that had bronze statues; gilt rococo furniture; and a crystal chandelier hanging from a black glass ceiling. It looked like the set decorators had got their periods mixed up.

There was no-one around. The place had that empty feel that's unmistakable. Leastways, the ground floor had. I walked on down the hallway and through into a big living room that must have been all of forty feet long. The furnishings in here were just as bizarre as the rest of the place. Black walls, white furniture; that sort of thing.

I went all through the ground floor without finding anybody. There were big French doors in rear that gave on to a tiled terrace with a swimpool and the garden beyond. The windows here were made of one-way glass so that you could look out on to the terrace but people outside couldn't see in.

I couldn't find a staircase but there was a mahogany door off the hallway. I opened it up. It was an elevator cage. It was marked I, Ground and Basement. I thumbed the button for the first floor and whined on up. I got out in a small corridor that was lined with doors. I tried the first. That was an empty bedroom.

I went on down the doors. There were two more bedrooms and a big room got up like a gymnasium with ropes, a vaulting horse and exercise frames. The last door I tried led to the biggest room of the house. It must have run the whole length. It was really two rooms with an archway connecting them.

The first part had a black glass floor, a white circular dining table and chairs to match. There were a few abstracts in white frames hanging on the walls. It all looked very expensive and very uncomfortable. I went on over to the white buffet which had bowls of wax fruit on it. That's how trendy the place was.

There was a black cupboard over the buffet. I opened the door. There was a dumb-waiter inside. I guessed it connected direct with the kitchen below. There was no sign of any feminine influence around so I figured Dr Eltz was a bachelor.

The other room at the far side of the alcove was a study of some sort. Or part business office. There were more of the black glass windows punched all along the front. In daylight there would have been a magnificent view over the ocean. I guessed this side of the house would face the same way as the terrace, the garden and the swimpool. I could see all the lights along the coast and chains of car-headlamps passing along the beach road. I stood and watched it for a couple of minutes. It was quite a spectacle.

Except for the interruption of the archway white fitted bookcases containing thousands of books ran around the other three walls. I took a few of the books down. They were mostly works on physiology, psychology and chemical engineering. A few cheap novels in gaudy paperback covers were jammed in among them. I put the books back with a sigh. It was a heavy case all right.

There was another alcove at the far end of the room. That had a desk, some grey steel filing-cabinets and more shelves containing rows of box files. There was a big white leather armchair with a high back standing to one side of the desk like it had been hurriedly pushed aside. It was turned away from the room toward the small fireplace and drawers in the desk were open. Some papers were strewn about the floor.

I stood and listened, a muscle fretting

in my cheek. I could hear an ambulance siren screaming from somewhere far off. I set fire to a cigarette and stared at the papers scattered on the floor. Then I got down on my knees behind the desk and rummaged around. I soon saw a professional had been at work.

There was nothing of any great interest here; some business receipts; a bill for dues from a professional body the doctor belonged to; some typed letters on matters affecting the Malmo Institute. I carried the letters over under the desk lamp to read. They were interesting but not relevant to my purpose.

I sighed and put them back on the floor where I found them. I went through the rest of the desk drawers. There was nothing there. As I stepped back I brushed against the white leather armchair. I must have been half-asleep this evening. It revolved slowly to face me.

Dr Eltz was dressed in a natty white suit with a blue shirt and tie to match.

A smile glinted in the black beard tinted with grey as he stared at me. I stepped back, started to make with my story. Then I looked closer. Something wasn't quite right. Dr Eltz' spread-out mustachio made him look more like a character out of Feydeau than ever. Except that this wasn't a farce.

I bent over to examine him more closely. I knew he was dead even before I saw the wire trace around his neck.

18

"**T**HEN there was one," I said heavily.

I stepped back from Eltz. It had been quite a moment and my belly muscles were still fluttering. So I guess I shouldn't have blamed myself too much. There came a low chuckle and a boot scraped the floor. I had my hand halfway to the Smith-Wesson butt when the large man stepped out from behind the drapes. He had a cannon in his hand big enough to have taken my head off at that range.

"How's the removal business?" I said.

He grinned. The curtains at the other side of the window billowed and shifted. A man in a blue wind-cheater stood there. The wire-trace artist.

"The gang's all here," I told him.

He scowled. He didn't seem to have

234

the same sense of humour. The second man was the dangerous one. He was rangily built and he moved like a wild animal. He came up toward me with blank, dead eyes in a blank, dead face. He had glossy black hair, a mouth that was a thin black line and eyes like pools of mud. His eyelids were quite lashless, which made him look even more curious. His eyebrows were so thin they looked like they'd been pencilled on.

He was about six feet tall and had the deep chest, broad shoulders and flat belly of a man in hard, trim condition. I decided not to mess with him. If I had a choice, that is.

"We'll have the popgun, Faraday," he said. "Else you get it now."

He had a low, hissing voice that completed the deadly effect. He must have scared the hell out of old ladies.

"That wouldn't be very sensible," I said. "If you kill everybody, how the hell will you ever find what you're looking for?"

"He's talking sense, Cranko," the big man who'd been driving the furniture truck said diffidently. The mud pools swivelled to take him in.

"Why don't you give him my address while you're at it?" Cranko said softly.

The big man with the cannon seemed to shrink and waver like he was a strip of paper blowing in the wind.

"Does it matter?" he said.

The man in the windcheater turned back patiently.

"It matters," he said.

He tapped his breast with a thin forefinger with a long nail and then went on to tap his forehead. It was a melodramatic gesture and I guess my admiration must have shown on my face.

"You got it here all right," he said, meaning the area of his heart. "But you lack it here."

"He means you're short on brains," I told the big man.

"I know what he meant," he said

236

good humouredly. "But I'd still like your cannon."

"Sure," I said.

I put my hand inside my jacket. Cranko was about three feet from me now. His breath hissed out of his mouth and he stopped suddenly. He froze in one of those weird positions characters on television are always adopting these days. He had his hand spread out like a chopping blade and his left foot way back behind the other. I tried not to show how impressed I was.

"Take it very easy, Faraday," Cranko said.

"I'm getting a bit bored with kung-fu," I said. "Even Bruce Lee's dead and he was the best of the lot."

The thin man's breath whistled in his throat.

"If my foot catches you underneath the chin your neck will snap like a stick of rotten celery," he said. "Do I make myself clear?"

"Perfectly," I told him. "With that stance you could even break a stick of

237

good celery. Is that Pose 127 or 135? I haven't got to that part of the book yet."

The big man with the pistol chuckled. I guess he was the straight man normally and my dialogue made a break for him.

"Just drop it on the floor," Cranko said.

I got the gun and held it barrel down, my finger tips on the extremities of the butt. I held it up so both men could see it. Then I let it drop. It bounced on the carpet and finished up near the thin man's feet. He bent swiftly, like a cat, and scooped it up. He looked at it critically.

"A .38," he said. "Not as good as a Magnum."

"It suits me," I said. "It would stop you all right."

The thin man smiled. It was a deadly thing to look at. He crossed over and put the Smith-Wesson on the desk. The big man stood and watched me. The pistol didn't waver a fraction so I didn't try anything. Cranko came back toward me.

"Let's see how good you are, man to man," he said.

He adopted a pose and his hand came through the air toward me with fantastic speed, the edge of the palm like a chopping blade. I backed away and while I was doing that his right foot came up as he pirouetted. It was so close I felt the wind of his shoe as he passed. He was right. My neck would have been snapped if it had landed. The thin man laughed. I'd gotten a chair between us by this time.

"Cut it out," the big man said urgently. "This is no time for horsing around."

He waved the pistol in the thin man's direction.

"For once I agree with you," I said.

The thin man stared at me, his face expressionless.

"These characters are all the same," he said. "Hand to hand and they can't take it."

"Just like Mackensen and Eltz," I said. "Face to face. From behind with a wire trace."

Cranko's face turned a dull muddy colour to match his eyes. He made an abrupt step toward me. The big man came forward, got between us.

"Forget it," he told Cranko urgently. "We've more important things to attend to. There'll be time for that later."

"Not if I'm conscious there won't," I said.

The big man looked at me. Up close his face wasn't unsympathetic.

"You may not be conscious, Mr Faraday," he said simply. "That was a pretty good play you made, getting out of the truck like that."

He spoke as one professional to another.

"Hard on the hands," I said. "Still, it's better than riding on Ghost Trains with our friend here."

"Ask the man what he means," Cranko said in a dead voice.

"I was up at Funland," I said. "I

saw you give Mackensen the big chill. Leastways, I got to him just three minutes too late."

There was an ugly silence. The eyes of the man in the windcheater were like the sockets of dead eyes as he stared at me. The big man gave a jarring laugh.

"You just signed your death-warrant, buddy."

I laughed too.

"I did that as soon as I walked in here. You don't think Cranko would have let me walk out anyway, do you?"

The big man rubbed his chin with the muzzle of the pistol. He looked baffled.

"I guess not," he said, as though I'd just explained an abstruse point in mathematics for him.

"Which is why I'm safe all the while I've got The Zetland Method," I said.

There was another explosive silence. Cranko came forward, found himself up against the barrel chest of the big pug. The big man was smiling now.

"Well, Mr Faraday, that makes a difference. We could whip it out of you."

I went over and sat down on the chair where I could keep the big man between me and Cranko.

"You could," I admitted. "But that takes time. And that's one thing you haven't got."

The big man lowered the pistol slightly. His face was deep in what for him passed as thought.

"We could offer you money."

"That would be very nice," I told him. "Except that I couldn't spend it all while I'm dead."

The thin man made an ugly sucking sound. It seemed to go with the tableau in the room somehow.

"Supposing you just get on the phone to your principal?" I said. "He'll know how to take it on from here."

The big man got quickly in Cranko's way. I couldn't see the thin man's face but it must have looked ugly. Even the big man had an expression like I'd slapped him across the nostrils.

"You know too much for your own good, Faraday," he gritted.

"Does it make any difference?" I said.

The big man shrugged. He turned back to Cranko.

"We might as well do as he says."

★ ★ ★

I sat forward on the chair and set fire to my second cigarette. The big man sat on Eltz's desk with his back to the shelves and looked at me curiously. I wouldn't have recognised him without the coveralls, he looked so different. He held the pistol slackly in his lap, the muzzle down toward the floor. I'd measured the chances but the distance was too great. He would have blasted me before I'd covered a yard.

Today the big man wore a pearl-grey suit with a Hawaiian open-neck shirt that showed his strong neck muscles. He looked hard and durable. I'd have to depend on him for a break if I wanted to come out on my feet. I knew I couldn't rely on anything but a quick death from the kung-fu expert if he cut loose. He'd presumably gone down to the ground floor to phone. He seemed a hell of a time.

The big man relaxed the corners of his mouth and looked at me humorously.

"You're in a tough business, mister," he said.

I feathered out blue smoke and watched it ascend to the study ceiling.

"It's a living," I said.

His smile widened a crack.

"Or a death," he said.

I shrugged.

"The game's not over yet."

"It is for you," he said simply.

"What do they call you?" I asked.

"Tiny."

He grinned again. With his hard, sun-burned features and the brown eyes with the very bright pupils he looked like some scuba-diving expert who gave lectures at summer camps. I heard the whine of the elevator coming back then. Tiny heard it too. He got up off the desk with a remarkably quick movement for such a big man.

"Stay put," he rasped.

He went over to the archway separating the two rooms and looked anxiously across the dining room area. I realised then for the first time how vulnerable the two men were here in a house that wasn't their own and with an unexplainable corpse in the armchair. Tiny must have guessed it too because he told Cranko, "We ought to get moving."

The thin man appeared in the arch next to the big character.

"What did he say?"

Cranko looked at me with his dead eyes.

"We do it any way we like," he said

245

deliberately. "But we get that slip of paper."

He crossed over toward me. I stood up and tensed myself. The big man came quickly behind Cranko. His brown eyes looked worried.

"I got a better idea," he said. "Like the shamus said we got no time to hang around here."

Cranko turned to face him. He looked like a ballet dancer with his slim figure and air of suppressed tension.

"It better be a good suggestion," he said.

"It is," Tiny told him.

He looked at me derisively.

"Faraday's used to being knocked around. If he clams up there's nothing we can do to open his mouth. But he's not so keen on getting the ladies slapped about."

Cranko's dead eyes came briefly to life.

"So?" he said in that curiously soft voice.

"So this," the big man said. "We go

246

take the Hopcroft girl apart. Or maybe that blonde secretary of his."

Cranko put his head on one side and looked at me critically.

"You mean to say a gumshoe like this rates a secretary?" he said.

Tiny looked at me blankly.

"You better make up your mind."

"I already made it up," I said. "The formula's in a safe deposit box in L.A. here. It's just a lot of figures on a piece of paper."

The big man's face expressed satisfaction. Cranko looked disappointed.

"What's your suggestion, Faraday?" Tiny said. "We can't get the document till morning," I said. "The bank doesn't open until ten. I'll go down and get it for you."

Tiny nodded. He looked at Cranko.

"Guess you better go make another phone call." He waited until the thin man had quitted the room. "It's a deal, Faraday. We go down to the bank in the morning. In the meantime we hole up somewhere for the night."

He waved the pistol. I walked over through the archway in the direction of the elevator.

"It's all right with me," I said. "It's better than being dead."

19

WE rode down in the elevator. Tiny's pistol was jammed in my back so I didn't try anything. We got out on the ground floor. I walked in front of the big man down the corridor and into the living room which had black walls and white furniture. There were a lot of lamps with white Swedish paper shades burning in here but the place still looked dark. I went and sat on a white plastic divan that felt as uncomfortable as it looked.

Cranko was sitting near a burnished steel fireplace staring at the yellow Swedish telephone like he'd never seen one before. He had his chin on his hands and he seemed like he was in the Third State of Nirvana. Or whatever it is that kung-fu experts have. He gave a start when Tiny backed down the room toward him. The big man still kept the pistol fanned in my direction so I stayed put.

"All set?" the big man said.

Cranko nodded. His dead insect eyes raked over the big man and then on to me.

"I spoke to the man," he said. "He sounded pleased. He said to follow through."

Tiny nodded with satisfaction.

"So we go down to the bank in the morning," he said.

Cranko nodded again.

"Sure," he said. "Then I get to . . ."

"We know all about that," the big man interrupted him. "Just use your head. Remember, we've got to hang around with this character all night before we pick up the formula. Your attitude won't help to keep him around."

Cranko looked at the big man's cannon.

"That will," he said.

"Don't mind about me," I told them.

"I'm having a great time. I can hardly wait to see Bruce Lee do some more of his exercises. I'll bet he snaps a bread stick before breakfast just to keep himself in condition."

The big man smiled happily. The blank eye-sockets swivelled to take me in. Cranko's face had a baffled look.

"He's got style, I'll say that for him," he said grudgingly.

"Sure," Tiny said. "And now we get the hell out of here."

I got up as the two men came over to join me. Tiny kept the cannon steady on my gut. We went through the hallway and out the front door. Tiny kept close in behind me so that no-one on the street could see the pistol. Not that there was anyone around anyway.

"We got a problem," Tiny said as we got up to the dark sedan in the driveway.

He stood thinking for a moment while we both waited. They were pretty cool characters. I noticed they'd locked the front door behind us. It might be some time before Eltz was found. By that time they'd have finished their business.

"You'd better take Faraday's heap," Tiny said at last.

He looked at me.

"Give him your keys."

I passed them to Cranko.

"Take it easy," I said. "I just got four new tyres."

Cranko didn't say anything. His eye-sockets looked past me like his thoughts were far away.

"You sure you can handle him?" he asked the big man. "He might jump you if you're taking the wheel."

"I could give you my parole," I said. "Or I could ride in back."

Tiny didn't exactly laugh but he came close to it.

"Sure," he said. "And I could play solo fiddle at the Hollywood Bowl."

I sighed.

"It was a good try, anyway," I said.

Cranko went off down the drive. The big man waved the cannon and I got behind the wheel.

He got in beside me and passed over the keys. The pistol barrel was very steady on my gut.

"Drive," he said.

I drove.

★ ★ ★

It had been a rough night. We had stopped off at a small motel up in the foothills to the north. There were two bedrooms. I slept in my clothes on one of the beds while Cranko and Tiny took it in turns to guard me. They had a tray sent to the cabin from the motel restaurant so we didn't starve. Which was something under the circumstances.

But they kept the room light on so I didn't get much sleep. I woke up every hour or so to find one of them sitting in a chair about three feet from the bed, cannon turned toward me, watching with unblinking eyes. They were good pros as far as that went; I'd give them

253

that. I woke around five a.m. feeling like my mouth was full of steel-wool.

I lit a cigarette and feathered smoke at the ceiling. Cranko was on duty so I didn't waste any time in speaking. I just lay and smoked and watched the ceiling and thought about nothing, while the grey dawn light slowly strengthened to gold. They had all the blinds drawn but I could see by the quality of the light that it was misty, like it often is in the early morning in California this time of the year.

Presently I stubbed out the cigarette in the tray at the side of the bed and slept again. I didn't wake up until half-past seven this time. Tiny was sitting by the bed. He nodded.

"We're having breakfast around half-past eight," he said. "In case you want to freshen up."

I thanked him and got up from the bed. All my joints were aching and I had that stale, deadly feeling one always has after sleeping in one's clothes.

"All right to use the bathroom?" I said.

Tiny nodded. His eyes didn't leave my face.

"Sure," he said. "There's no way out that way. But leave the door open."

I walked on over and switched on the bathroom light. I didn't waste much time at the mirror. I looked worse than I figured. I didn't have a razor so I couldn't do much about the stubble. I rummaged around in the bathroom cabinet and found an old cut-throat in a leather case, probably left behind by a guest. I debated for a couple of minutes but decided against.

I kicked out of my clothes and got under the shower, swivelling under the hot jets and pummelling the staleness of the night away with the motel's jasmine soap. I dried myself on the warm, rough towel that was hung over the electric radiator and felt I might live. Until we'd been to the bank at any rate. I couldn't see Tiny; he hadn't moved from the bedside, except to swivel his chair toward the bathroom door, but I could see his shadow on the bedroom carpet so I knew he wasn't far away.

I got dressed and combed my hair and found I looked fairly presentable. I knotted my tie, re-wound my wrist watch and stepped into my shoes. I was just tying the laces when another shadow fell across the bathroom tiles. It was Cranko; his dead face looked expressionless.

"I'd like to use the facilities if you've finished," he grunted.

"Sure," I said. "Don't slip on the soap and break your neck."

Cranko grunted again.

"That'll be the day," he said.

He was wearing a white shirt and trousers and he pirouetted suddenly, his right foot coming round with a deadly chopping motion. I'd already moved out through the door. Tiny was standing up, the cannon in his hand. There was a ring at the bell. He waved the gun.

"You get it," he said. "Just remember I'm right behind."

"As if I could forget," I told him.

There was a blonde number at the door with a smile so bright it made the sunlight look shabby. She had a number five in red wool on the right nipple of her sweater. It was all I could do to keep my hands off it.

"Five always was my favourite number," I said.

There was a faint pink on the girl's face. There was another girl, just as good-looking, with a motorised trolley in the background.

"Too many of you or we could take this up," the first girl said. "Three breakfasts as ordered."

She handed me the closed tray. The girl's white teeth sparkled as she looked me up and down.

"I like them clean-shaven," she said.

"I'm just growing this for a revival of The Count of Monte Cristo," I told her. I felt the insistent pressure of Tiny's cannon in my spine.

"It's been a lovely friendship," I said.

The girl giggled.

"If you want lunch in your room just let me know," she said.

"I'll do that," I told her.

I carried the tray in and closed the door. Tiny's face was set like stone.

"You nearly bought it then," he said.

"I was only being friendly," I told him.

I put the tray down on the table. I suddenly felt hungry. There was everything there from ham and eggs to hot coffee and buttered rolls. I sat down and started demolishing my share. Tiny couldn't eat because he had to watch me. I put the cover over the other plates and poured him a cup of coffee. I pushed it across to him.

"You're not such a bad character, Faraday," he said.

He drank the coffee with his left hand, keeping the cannon in his right.

"Sure," I said. "I'm just on the wrong side."

Cranko came back then. Tiny put the pistol away and slid his own plate over. The thin man looked at me.

"You know what I can do with my bare hands," he said. "So we put the gun away and eat breakfast like civilised people."

"Some of us are civilised people," I told him. "It's the others who need to watch their manners."

Tiny's eyes regarded me curiously. Cranko didn't say anything. He picked up his plate and took a chair over near the door, where he could keep tabs on me. When breakfast was over I felt I might hold out. Until ten a.m. anyway.

"You'd better make that phone-call," Tiny told Cranko. "Then we move. We'll wait in the heap."

Cranko nodded.

"Just watch him," he grunted. "It's your turn to pick up the tab."

I got up and walked through into

the garage. I slid behind the wheel without waiting to be told. Tiny got in beside me and handed me the keys. I drove to the entrance. Tiny handed me the money to pay the bill. He took the ignition keys away and kept the pistol low down on the car seat, so the girl at the reception desk couldn't see anything unusual. By the time we got the receipt Cranko had re-joined us. He climbed in back.

"All set," he grunted to the big man.

We drove back into town. I found the nearest parking area to my branch of the Chase National and we walked back a couple of blocks. I got in a queue for one of the teller's cages with Tiny behind me.

"They may want to check," I said.

Tiny's eyes were like frozen water.

"What does that mean?"

"Just routine," I said. "My secretary deposited the envelope. She signed the chit. They might want verification."

Tiny licked his lips.

"Look here, Faraday," he began. "If there's any slip-ups . . . "

"There won't be from my end," I said. "They might want her signature as well as mine."

I was beginning to enjoy myself now. Tiny gave a strangled grunt. He had a hunted look on his face and he glanced across to Cranko.

"You better get that envelope."

"I'll do my best," I told him.

I could have got the envelope without any trouble. It was in my deposit box. And I'd got identification and my own key. All it wanted was my signature on the receipt. I'd numbered the envelope so there would be no problem identifying it. But Tiny didn't know that. In the event I wanted the bank to phone Stella. That way she would know something was wrong, that the fake formula was being removed.

She might want to speak to me. But these characters couldn't allow that. I figured Stella would know the score straight away. But whether she could do anything about it was another matter. It was a slim chance. But it was about the only one I had for the moment. The big man at my side in the queue would have to eliminate me. Even if he were reluctant Cranko wouldn't hesitate.

The clerk was helpful. I explained what I wanted and filled in the form. He smiled and tapped the document with his forefinger. I didn't know him and I figured he might want verification.

"It will take about ten minutes, sir. In the meantime if we could just get a check . . ."

"Sure," I said. "Just phone my secretary."

I gave him my office number and my driver's licence. He took them both away. Tiny's face was set like concrete.

"If this is a stall . . ." he hissed.

"Just relax," I told him. "You wanted the envelope. I didn't make the bank rules."

We waited a long ten minutes. I

could feel sweat trickling down inside my shirt collar. Tiny looked round once or twice like he could see security guards closing in on him. Beads of perspiration were shining among the roots of his hair. He had his hand in his inside pocket but I could feel the unmistakable pressure of the muzzle of the cannon against my side. Cranko hadn't moved from his position near the door. His nerves must have been like steel cables.

The clerk came back after about a hundred years. He was all smiles. The young lady had made the verification. He handed me the envelope. I signed the receipt and we walked out. Cranko fell in behind as we got to the door. We went back to the sedan. I handed Tiny the envelope. He exchanged a long glance with Cranko.

"What now?" I said.

"We take another little drive," Cranko said.

I got behind the wheel for the last time.

20

THE wheels of the black sedan rumbled as I pulled it on to the bluff and over on to the secondary road. Dust rose in choking clouds. It made me realise it hadn't rained for twenty-four hours. I was out of touch. It seemed like years since I'd walked into Eltz' house. Tiny had shut the car window and sweat glistened on his forehead. The muzzle of the big cannon was lined steadily on my gut.

I noticed then it was a Magnum. A slug from that would have torn my head clean off my shoulders at that close range. I didn't aim to give Tiny an excuse to use it. I glanced in the mirror. There was nothing on the road behind us. Cranko was sitting with his eyes half-closed but I could see by his position on the seat that he was poised ready to go into action in a fraction of a second.

I had thought I might slam the car into the nearest telephone pole but Tiny could have pulled the trigger and recovered control before the sedan left the road. We were only doing forty miles an hour. That was Cranko's instruction; he wasn't doing anything that would draw attention to the sedan or its progress across the city.

I knew where we were going now. There might be a chance of trying something once we got there. Like always I'd just have to play it by ear. I wondered what Stella would have done after getting the call from the bank. There wasn't much she could do. Unless Dobbs and his boys had gone to my office. They could get a description of Tiny from the teller at the Chase National.

Not that that would help. Unless Stella remembered my description of the man in the furniture van who'd jumped me near Marion Hopcroft's place. That seemed like years ago too. I turned again, on to another road that snaked up the hillside. We zig-zagged round the bends in low gear; there wasn't much traffic on the road and I had time to admire the scenery.

The Pacific looked a pale green today and it broke in splintered white fragments like glass along the brownish-gold sand. There were a lot of people horsing around in the water and a few sailboats jockeying for position farther out. The beach-road looked choked with automobiles. A long way out a big white pleasure liner was cruising, looking ghostly and insubstantial in the faint mist. It was a lot to leave if one had to leave. I gave it a long, hard look.

"You know where we're going, shamus?" Cranko said.

It was the first time he had spoken since the drive began.

"Sure," I said. "We're going to shoot a few frames of pool and then drink a couple of cool beers together."

266

Come to think of it a couple of Coors wouldn't have been half-bad on a day like this. Normally I'm not much of a one for drinking in the morning. But I'd make an exception in this case. And it was after midday. Tiny gave me a twisted smile.

"No pool, no beers," he said.

"That's a pity," I said.

I looked at Cranko in the mirror. His slit mouth hardly moved when he spoke. "I'll have one for you when we get back in," he said tonelessly.

"I'll look forward to it," I told him. I looked at Tiny's set face and then back at Cranko's in the mirror. He was sitting up now, with his hands spread out on the cushions on either side of him. I tensed myself, expecting his boot through the leather of the seat any moment.

"The Ghost Train again?" I said.

Tiny shook his head.

"Nothing fancy for a private eye," he said.

I clicked my teeth.

267

"Over the cliff?"

Tiny shrugged.

"Something like that," he said. "An accident. We'll play it by ear."

He put the gun muzzle forward.

"You know where to park. No funny stuff."

I pulled the sedan over toward the familiar iron gates. Inside the big hoop of white bulbs, the red neon spelled out: FUNLAND.

★ ★ ★

I slotted the sedan in between two other vehicles and killed the motor. I gave the keys to Tiny. I heard Cranko shift over on the cushions behind me. I watched him in the mirror. He got out the car and slammed the door. He came along to my door and opened it. Tiny put the pistol in his pocket but kept his hand on the butt.

He waited until I got out and then leaned over and locked the door. Cranko stood a yard away from me. I ignored him. I waited until Tiny closed his own door and came around the rear of the sedan. I looked at the neon of Funland, the circulating crowds. I couldn't see any help there. I went over to the rail and looked at the sea and the sky. There was a lot of it.

"Beautiful day, ain't it?" Tiny said. He sounded regretful.

"They don't come any better in Southern California," I said.

"You'll be spouting poetry next," Cranko sneered.

"I could do that too," I told him.

"You'd make a good pair of book-ends," Cranko said, looking from me to the big man and then back again. I looked inquiringly at Tiny.

"Where to?"

Tiny jerked his head.

"The other side the car-park. You'll find a gate there."

I followed the railing down, keeping in front of the parked automobiles. There didn't seem to be anyone around.

Tiny walked a yard behind me, his hand in his pocket. Cranko was out to the right now, behind the cars, guarding the flank. They'd chosen the place well. There were no more empty spaces this side, so no people. All the empty slots were up the far end. It didn't look like my day.

I found the white-painted picket-gate like Tiny said. I opened it. It led to a metalled path that led downhill between belts of trees and shrubbery. Tiny moved up behind me and I felt the insistent prod of the pistol barrel.

"Don't try anything," he said. "This only lasts a hundred yards."

I soon saw what he meant. The trees thinned away and we went through another gate. Cranko had re-joined Tiny now and they both walked a few paces behind. We were out on open meadowland, dotted with clumps of trees and outcrops of rock. The slope was a steep one and went down to the cliffs in rear of the beach. I knew the set-up. It didn't make me feel any better.

"Farther along," Cranko grunted. "The fencing gives out. It will look more natural."

"Like hell it will," I said.

We walked a couple of hundred yards along the turf, skirting outcrops of rock and threading between groves of trees. There was no cover here that was practical against two armed men, even if I could have broken away. The slope was pretty steep here and I turned to look up at the sky-line. I turned back quickly and stumbled, knocking against Cranko. He rounded on me, snarling.

"Take it easy," I said. "It was an accident."

Tiny got between us; his big back blocked out the slope. He urged me forward. We were only a couple of yards from the cliffs. They fell sheer for a couple of hundred feet to broken ground in back of the beach road. I paused to watch a hang-glider circling lazily in the far distance. I looked at

Cranko, saw the red and yellow stripes drawing near.

A great shadow swept across the ground. Cranko turned like a snake. I rammed my fist against Tiny's belly then, heard the breath expelled in pain. He cannoned into the thin man and they went down in a tangle of arms and legs. I was already running in a zig-zag up the slope as the hang-glider passed low overhead. The youth strapped into the harness looked down in amazement as the shot slammed out. It spanged off a boulder as I pounded uphill to where the long line of people spread out across the turf.

They carried gliders of all shapes and sizes and the babble of conversation came down like surf beating on the shore. I was in among the first of them now. I saw Cranko and Tiny running like madmen up the slope but I'd got a hundred yards start. I wouldn't get another chance like this. Already the next glider was being launched from a flat shelf of rock. I made for it.

The scarlet kite-shape wing looked beautiful and elemental lying on the rocky surface, the lightweight aluminium tubing glinting in the sun. I pushed my way through, fighting down a rising wave of panic. Cranko and the big man were lost in the waves of excited enthusiasts. There wouldn't be time to strap myself in. I shoved the two teenage kids aside, sent them sprawling. Angry shouts arose.

I already had the triangle-shaped framework in my hands. I ran clumsily to the edge of the bluff. The slope blurred and shimmered before me. I gulped and hurled myself outward. My momentum took me clear of the rock. My heels made a sickening scraping noise and then the slope was rushing past me, a vast green blur.

The kite-glider gave a heart-stopping lurch and then I had shifted my grip and the motion became steadier. The slap of the shot came a second later but it must have gone wide. I could see Cranko and Tiny far below, out the

right-hand corner of my eye so I must
have been banking. I shifted my weight
again, found the machine responding.

We were at the main cliff edge,
the sea a dazzling green before me.
I looked down through my dangling
legs, felt sick. I concentrated on the
horizon. The wind up here seemed like
a hurricane. The scarlet nylon above
me vibrated in the sunlight and looked
as frail as gossamer. Now I only wanted
to get down as soon as possible.

But not here. Not over the road with
its racing automobiles. I was clear now
and my height down to three hundred
feet. The golden strip of beach drifted
lazily by. I had a better idea then.
I shifted my weight slightly again,
turning the machine over the sea. I
knew where I was. There was a curved
headland in front which jutted out into
the water.

Just the place for a convenient death.
If I could swim a few hundred yards
under water and get round the point
without being spotted. It depended

how broken the water was. I hoped the people on the beach would concentrate on the spot where the glider went in.

The white buildings of L.A. shimmered in the far distance. The green water was coming up fast now as I deliberately lost height. I waited a few more seconds. I couldn't have been airborne more than a minute but a lot seemed to be happening. I was low enough.

I waited another ten seconds. It was notoriously difficult to judge one's height over water. I let go the aluminium tubing. I hit the water in a cloud of glittering spray and went down into darkness.

21

"YOU must be crazy," Stella said.

She looked at me with concern, tooling her car up off the beach-road.

"I'm alive at any rate," I said. "And thanks for the dry clothes."

Stella gave me a tight smile. The gold bell of her hair shimmered in the afternoon sunshine.

"I knew something was badly wrong when I got the call from the bank," she said. "But I couldn't do anything about it."

"It's all right, honey," I said. "It worked out just fine."

"But a hang-glider, Mike," Stella said. "You might have been killed."

I grinned.

"You don't seem to get the situation, honey. I sure as hell would have been killed if I'd hung around on top of the cliff. As it was I almost blacked out when I hit the water. I dropped off too high."

"You're sure those characters think you're dead?" Stella said.

I nodded, slipping my salt-stained trousers down over my knees. I was in the rear of the car changing, so Stella couldn't see what I was doing.

"I swam round behind the point. I got in among the rocks. I hit the beach again about a mile farther down. I got on the highway and thumbed a lift back to where I could find a pay-booth."

Stella turned the car on to the secondary road, a frown on her face.

"Even so, Mike, you're taking a risk. If they know you're alive you won't last five minutes."

I shook my head, pulling on a fresh pair of pants.

"They won't find me until I'm ready to hit. And that bluff was over a mile from the beach. All they'd have been able to see from there was me going in the water. Nothing else. And don't forget there was a haze . . . "

"All right, Mike," Stella interrupted. "You've made your point. Where now?"

"We pick up my heap," I said. "Then we wait until after dark. I've got one more call to make to wrap this up."

Stella pulled the car in through the motel entrance as I put my hand on her shoulder. It seemed like a year since I'd been there. The Buick was still in the driveway where Cranko had left it. I stayed in the car and put on a fresh jacket. I transferred my sodden wallet to it.

Stella got out the car and went over to the Buick. She came back in a few moments.

"They left the keys in it."

She handed them to me.

"Fine," I told her. "That takes care of that. Now I'll want another pistol from my place."

"I'd better go on over and get that,

Mike," Stella said. "It would be safer. I can take your wet things as well."

She fingered my sodden wallet with disgust.

"We'll have to get you a new social security card."

I grinned again.

"I should have carried more insurance. There's little social security in my racket."

I gave Stella my house-keys and she gave me some new bills from her handbag to replace those which were stuck together with sea-water. She got in the passenger seat opposite me in back while I finished my toilet. I was decent now. She took the bills between slim fingers.

"I'll dry these out at the office."

She put them away in her bag and got out the car. She went over toward the motel reception desk. She came back in five minutes.

"They checked out all right. I thought they might have come back."

I stared at her.

"Tiny and Cranko. Not them."

Stella shook her head and got in the car again.

"It's been done," she said mysteriously. "Never neglect even the unlikely."

"Yes, Mrs. Holmes," I said.

Stella leaned forward and kissed me gently on the side of the face. It sent up my blood-count a lot.

"I wanted to see the Hopcroft girl," I said. "But there isn't time in my schedule. We'd better make it tomorrow."

Stella leaned forward. Her blue eyes searched my face.

"You'd better let me know your movements."

I told her where I intended to go and what I intended to do. She looked dubious but she didn't say anything.

"No news from Dobbs?"

Stella shook her head.

"They'll be around when they're ready," I said. "I'd just like to wrap this up first."

"Where do we meet, Mike?" Stella said. "So I can give you the gun."

"Your place at six," I said. "It will be safer. I'm going to use the afternoon getting a good bath and a meal."

Stella nodded. "Take care. You had one bath already."

"Sure," I said.

I got out the car and went over to my own heap. She'd already gunned out before I got the key in the ignition. I started making time across town.

* * *

It was just after seven when I got to the house. It was up a canyon on the edge of town so it was nice and private. It was raining slightly again so I carried a light raincoat. I had a reason. If I was going up against two or three I wanted to hit first and plan my own way out. On my feet. I didn't intend to take any chances with Cranko.

I'd checked on the Luger. It was oiled and fully loaded but it was a big,

281

clumsy thing. I didn't really want it bu
Stella had brought the wrong gun. Sh
was so helpful I didn't say anythin
about it. At least it would do almo
as much damage as a Magnum at clo
range. And I'd be working close in.
pulled the Buick over under the shado
of a tall hedge and killed the motor.

I figured I was still two or thre
hundred yards from my destination an
I didn't want to advertise my presenc
I'd like to have seen the reaction whe
they'd opened the envelope. For all
knew The Zetland Method might hav
been the formula for a new hair rin
from the figures I'd given them.

I stubbed out my cigarette in th
dash-tray and got out the car. I walke
back down the cement sidewalk. It w
badly eroded and I almost stumble
when I got up close to the house.
There was a lamp burning here atop
a long pole. There was a big crack
in the sidewalk where the hillside
was falling away; it reminded me of
the impermanence of everything in

was a pity about having to spoil it.
But I guess it was a cheap out if it
came to the push. I eased up on to the
porch, making sure there was no-one
around.

The front door was on the latch
eased it open and slipped throug
was in a big hall with a numbe
doors opening up off it. Ligh
spilling from a half-open door
end to the right of a staircase.
until my eyes adjusted to the
here. The low murmur of v
coming from the doorway.
safety-catch of the Luge
held it barrel down benea
raincoat. I caught sight
a gilt-framed mirror; i
natural to me.

I got up close to th
and stopped. There
point in hanging
drop this time.
of Cranko. I c
men in the roo
There appeare

The unfamiliar one was doing most of the talking.

"I don't know why I employed you," it said.

"Because you hadn't the guts to do your own strong-arm work," a second voice said.

I grinned. I recognised Cranko.

"This is one hell of a mess whichever way you look at it," the other voice went on.

"Only if you panic," Cranko said. "Mackensen won't talk. Eltz has gone, sure. But that could be just another hippie murder."

The other voice broke into a sort of yelp.

"Don't you characters realise that this is liable to focus interest on the Malmo Institute?"

"That's your problem," Tiny's voice said sullenly. "You hired us to do a job when you botched things yourself. We done it and now you don't like it."

"I'm not ungrateful," the third voice

said. "But the result is zero and we've got a lapful of corpses to explain."

"What did you expect us to do?" Tiny said. "We were going through his desk when he walked in. Cranko had no choice."

"You're sure Faraday is dead," the third voice said.

I moved closer.

"We hung around for an hour," Cranko said. "He didn't come up."

I stepped through the doorway.

"You didn't wait long enough," I said.

★ ★ ★

There was a long, empty silence. The room was a library. Tiny was sitting in a big chair at the far side from me. Behind him were long drapes partly concealing French windows. Cranko was sitting on the edge of a big walnut desk over at one side. His eyes were quite expressionless as he looked at me. I leaned against the doorjamb holding the raincoat and trying to look casual. The red-haired man behind the desk turned an ashen colour.

"Don't let me interrupt you, Dr Snell," I said. "You were doing all right before I came in."

Cranko was the first to recover himself. He sat easily, almost insolently on the desk and looked at me as though he was pleased to see me. He shook his head wonderingly.

"I thought I'd been robbed of a pleasure, Faraday. I see I was wrong. You must be made of cast iron."

"I do my best to survive," I said modestly. "Anybody else in the house?"

I looked at Snell, who shook his head. His face was regaining its normal inflamed colour. His features looked more neutral than when I'd last seen him and his sandy hair hung down over the collar of his flowered dressing gown. He kept his hands in his pockets to conceal the trembling of his fingers.

"I heard you were dead," he said in a none too steady voice.

"You heard wrong," I said. "I'm a good underwater swimmer."

"You got out twice," Tiny said. "It won't happen a third time."

"You don't think I'd come here like this without taking precautions," I said.

Cranko got up swiftly. I tightened my grasp on the Luger.

"You'd better look around," he told Tiny. He smiled at me.

"With your permission?"

"Why not?" I said.

Tiny went over to the French windows and disappeared; he came back in two minutes. He looked at me and shook his head.

"No-one around," he said.

Snell smiled slightly.

"You want to do a deal, Mr Faraday? You've still got The Zetland Method, that it?"

I saw a sudden sharp look pass between Cranko and Tiny. I knew the score then. I jumped in quickly.

"Before we make a deal I want to

get a few things straight. Just for the record. Like all the top brass in the Malmo Institute you knew what Professor Hopcroft was working on. You wanted The Zetland Method."

Snell nodded slowly.

"Sure, Mr Faraday. It was worth a fortune. I boned up on it in some material the old fool was indiscreet enough to publish in one of the technical magazines."

"Mackensen was incorruptible so you and Eltz went into partnership together?" I said. "But Hopcroft wouldn't play. So you waited until he'd finished his work and then ran him down on the boulevard one night. That way you hoped to find the formula at your leisure. Only he'd hidden it pretty well."

Snell swallowed. His eyes had gone a muddy colour. Cranko stood by the desk examining his nails. Tiny had gone to sit down in the armchair again. If he had his cannon on him he'd kept it well hidden.

289

"That's about the size of it," Snell said.

"You could kill an old man and make it look like a hit and run," I said. "But you and Eltz were out of your class so you employed a couple of pros."

Snell shrugged.

"It seemed like a good idea at the time. Only, somehow, Mackensen got wise to what was going on. We had to work fast."

"Why Funland?" I said.

Snell smiled.

"That was a good touch. I knew Mackensen suspected me. But he thought Eltz was on the square. He was worried about the set-up. So Eltz suggested an informal meeting at the fairground one evening, when they could talk freely and without being observed. Mackensen lived not very far from there and it was a natural place to meet."

I grinned.

"And there was me looking for all

sorts of complicated explanations. You killed Eltz so you wouldn't have to split."

Snell nodded.

"Partly that. Things got more involved as we went along. I thought Eltz might have got the formula himself. So I had Cranko here call on him. But his elimination wasn't planned. Now I see its advantages. He knew I'd run down Hopcroft. And I shan't have to share."

"You got these boys to get me away from my house with a fake message to meet at the restaurant," I said. "When you didn't come up with anything they were to beat it out of me. And you're still no further forward."

Snell stood up. "I wouldn't say that, Mr Faraday. I know you've got The Zetland Method. And I intend to have it."

"Why don't you wise up," I said. "Cranko's got the formula. I went down to the bank and drew it out this morning. But I guess they didn't tell you that."

Tiny rose with an abrupt movement as Snell reached in the drawer of the desk. His face was distorted with rage as he came up with the cannon. I fired twice through the raincoat as Cranko came wheeling across the carpet, his arms and legs held out rigid like a catherine wheel. His body shuddered as the bullets ploughed through.

The glass of the French windows smashed and I went down as the room filled with smoke and flame.

22

CRANKO collapsed like a rag doll against the far wall. He was coughing blood, his whole body shuddering. Tiny went down with a crash, a red stain spreading out on his jacket. I crawled away behind the desk as splinters rained from the parquet floor near my face. Snell swayed, the big cannon coming up slowly, almost casually. A black hole spread out on his forehead, blue-rimmed, then filling with blood.

The gun dropped from his fingers as the massive, sheet-iron face of Sprowle eased through the door. He beamed at me happily.

"Thought you might like some help, Mr Faraday."

I went to sit alongside the desk and reached for a cigarette with shaky fingers. Snell fell back against the wall, leaving black smears along it.

"Remind me to thank you when my nerves have recovered," I said.

Two big men in black suits came in the room, went out the door that led to the hall. They didn't look at me. I guess they were used to such Shakespearean finales. Sprowle came over to me and sat down on the desk. He kept his eye on Tiny, who was groaning in the corner. A tall figure in an elegant lightweight suit came through the window. Dobbs smiled thinly as he bent to light my cigarette with a silver lighter.

"Rather messy, Mr Faraday, but effective. I'm grateful to you."

"How did you get on to me?" I said.

Dobbs smiled again. He glanced bleakly over at Snell.

"It's not a question of us getting on to you. You've never been out of our sight since you left the motel."

"You cut it pretty fine," I said.

Dobbs shook his head.

"We were after the formula, Mr

Faraday. You were expendable so far as we were concerned."

The two big men came back in the room, looked incuriously at me.

"No-one else in the house," the first one said.

Dobbs nodded.

"Go wait in the car," he said.

I got up, my nerves settling. I put the Luger down on the desk and went over to Tiny. His eyes were clouded with pain. I took the Smith-Wesson out his inside pocket, kicked away the cannon he'd been using. I got him up to a divan, staunched his shoulder-wound with his handkerchief. Sprowle stood by the desk beaming. He looked at his pistol thoughtfully.

"I haven't lost my touch," he said.

"Who was the kung-fu merchant?" Dobbs said.

"A character called Cranko," I said. "Nasty. He's got my envelope."

Dobbs sat down on the desk and folded his arms like he was at a board-meeting.

"The Zetland Method," he said. "I'd like a look at that."

"Sure," I said.

I went over to Cranko and got the envelope out of his pocket. He was quite dead. The Luger had done a lot of damage.

"What was The Zetland Method?" I said.

"Is," Dobbs corrected me. "A petrol substitute, to put it simply. Worth billions."

I must have looked impressed because Sprowle gave an ear-splitting grin. I gave the envelope to Dobbs. He tore it open and examined the figures with a rapidly growing frown.

"This material is quite useless, Mr Faraday," he said in an even voice.

I put the Smith-Wesson back in my shoulder-holster, collected a pistol from Cranko and put it down on the desk between Dobbs and Sprowle. The giant stood and watched me without saying anything.

"So I told you," I said. "It was a

dummy I set up as bait for Snell. And he took it."

"But I don't take it, Mr Faraday," Dobbs said wearily. There was an icy edge to his voice.

"I don't know what you mean," I said.

I went over to stand near Tiny, where I could see Sprowle and Dobbs either side of the desk.

"Where's Cedric?" I said.

Sprowle smiled slowly.

"He was called away on business with Mrs Hart."

I looked around the room.

"He's better out of it," I said.

Sprowle looked at me happily.

"You can say that again."

"We're wasting time," Dobbs said.

"I told you the set-up," I said. "I kept my end of the bargain."

"So you did," Dobbs said with another thin smile.

He took out an envelope from the inside pocket of his grey suit and put it down on the desk.

"You'd better count it. It's all there. It's yours just as soon as we've finished our business."

"We've finished our business," I said. "My guess is Hopcroft took the details of the formula with him."

I tapped my forehead. "Up here."

Dobbs stirred audibly on the desk as though a cold wind had rippled through him.

"Come now, Mr Faraday. You surely don't expect me to believe that. How do I know there weren't two envelopes in the bank."

He looked at me with a stony face.

"And that you simply drew out the phoney."

I sighed. I looked from Sprowle to Dobbs and then back again.

"I'm telling the truth, Mr Dobbs. I haven't got The Zetland Method and I've never laid eyes on it. You don't want to face up to it. Neither did Mrs Hart when I mentioned it."

Dobbs looked at me regretfully.

"You don't understand, Mr Faraday.

The syndicate doesn't like failure. If you don't come through with the formula then I've failed as well. The syndicate wouldn't like that."

I nodded. I glanced down at Tiny. He was unconscious again but he was still breathing. The flow of blood had stopped. I looked at his cannon lying on the floor. It was too far away to do me any good. And it was useless trying to go for the Smith-Wesson.

"So they might rub you?" I said.

Dobbs drew in his breath with a sucking noise. Sprowle looked at him. There was surprise in his eyes. His sandpaper voice sounded low and husky.

"I reckon Mr Faraday's levelling, Mr Dobbs," he said.

"Nobody's asking you," Dobbs said evenly. "You provide the muscle around here. I'll do the thinking."

"If you give it to me how does that help you find Hopcroft's formula?" I said.

Dobbs gave a brief smile.

299

"It doesn't," he said. "But it gets me off the hook."

The lean, tanned face with the clipped mustache looked genuinely regretful. The blue eyes had never been more sincere. It was only the little scar at the right-hand corner of his mouth and the narrow, bleached line of the mouth itself that spoiled things.

"You got three seconds, Faraday," he said.

"Three hours wouldn't help," I said. "What I don't know I can't tell you."

Dobbs shook his head.

"That's your last word?"

"Pretty well if you intend to rub me," I said.

Sprowle looked at me closely. There was a strange expression on his face which I hadn't seen before.

"Time's up, Mr Faraday," Dobbs said.

He turned to the big man.

"Take care of it."

Sprowle looked at me, then at Dobbs.

He picked up Cranko's cannon from the desk.

"Don't you think we ought to . . ." he began.

Dobbs' voice had a steel edge to it now.

"Just take care of it," he said.

Sprowle picked the cannon up. His eyes looked sick and he licked his lips. Dobbs stared at me coldly.

"I feel sorry for you," I told him.

Sprowle brought the cannon up; its black mouth seemed to fill the whole room. I closed my eyes. The report seemed to take the top of my head off; the shock stung my cheeks and I thought my ear-drums had burst. I opened my eyes again. Dobbs was halfway across the desk, going down; the front of his suit was like a piece of raw meat. He looked incredulously at Sprowle. Blue smoke curled from the barrel of the cannon and the big man's hammered sheet-metal face was angry. Dobbs stood there like he was pinned to the air; then the hinges in his legs collapsed. He hit the desk top with his head, left a smear of blood on the surface and made the floor with a crash that seemed to shake the building.

"Thanks," I said.

Sprowle smiled slowly.

"You and me's pros," he said simply. "He had no call to do that."

He looked without regret at Dobbs on the floor.

"What made you change your mind?" I said.

Sprowle looked down at the cannon. Smoke was still coming from the muzzle.

"I just got tired of taking Dobbs' orders, I guess."

"The syndicate won't be pleased," I said.

Sprowle grinned. "If they know."

He looked thoughtfully round the room.

"Let us sit upon the ground and tell sad stories of the deaths of kings," he quoted.

I grinned.

"Not while those two gorillas outside are still around."

"I'll handle them," Sprowle said.

He got out his own pistol and put a shot through Cranko's body. It jerked crazily and splinters flew from the wall behind him. Sprowle went quickly over and put Tiny's cannon in Cranko's right hand. He was kneeling by Dobbs' body when footsteps sounded on the path. One of the big men looked in through the French doors.

"Cranko got Dobbs," Sprowle said briefly. "He wasn't quite dead. I finished him off."

The big man came over and looked down at what was left of Dobbs.

"Christ," he said quietly. "What do we do now?"

"Leave it to me," Sprowle said. "Just keep the motor running."

The big man looked at me and shrugged.

"Right," he said and went on out at the run. I heard the engine of the black sedan throb into life.

"Sorry to leave you with all this mess, Mr Faraday," Sprowle said.

"I'll manage," I said. "I always do."

Sprowle put out a big horny hand for me to shake.

"Guess I'll visit my brother in New York after this," he said.

"It might be advisable," I told him. "Mrs Hart might not buy your story."

Sprowle looked thoughtful.

"I hadn't thought of that."

I picked up the envelope from the desk and gave it to him.

"You'll need this."

His eyes opened wide. He fanned the C-notes.

"All this?"

"My life's worth more than that," I said.

He went out through the window so fast I hardly noticed him go. The car gunned out as I reached for the phone and dialled the police. I went over to look at Tiny. He'd make it all right. I heard a noise then. I got out the Smith-Wesson and went back in the corridor. I opened the door of the room the noise was coming from. There was a TV set going in the corner. Strange I hadn't heard it earlier. Unless one of the big goons had turned it on for something.

There was a news bulletin on. Something about the President's visit to New York. There was the usual motorcade and some shots of politicians on a platform. Something made me look closer. There was a woman sitting next but one to the President. I stared. It was Mrs Hart all right. The camera panned over the faces in close-up. A muscle twitched in my cheek.

Mrs Hart looked at ease like she did this every day of the week. She probably did come to that. Only Mrs Hart wasn't what the TV newscaster called her. I put the Smith-Wesson away and reached over and switched the set off.

I knew now that no-one would be able to get at the syndicate. Leastways, not those that mattered. I decided I wouldn't say anything about it. I went heavily back in the next room and sat down to wait for the police.

★ ★ ★

It was after nine o'clock when I got up to Marina Bluff. The housekeeper Anna let me in. I went up to the room on the first floor where we'd had dinner. It seemed like years ago. The girl was standing on the big balcony that was cantilevered out from the main house. The screens were pulled back and the night wind ruffled the curtains. There was a fine view of the lights of houses in the surrounding hills. I walked in quietly over the tiling. Anna hadn't announced me.

"The case is finished," I said. "Snell killed your father. But I guess you knew that already didn't you?"

The girl turned to face me. The wind ruffled her ash-blonde hair. Her green eyes were expressionless.

"Would you like a drink, Mike?"

306

she said gently. "Whisky on the table there."

I went over to the round table which was littered with the remains of dinner. I took one of the upended German crystal tumblers and poured out a good splash from the decanter. I carried it over to where the girl stood. She wore a scarlet silk dressing gown and she looked very small and vulnerable.

"We almost cleared out the Malmo Institute," I said. "They'll be needing a new set of top brass."

The girl went to sit down on the edge of one of the big lounging chairs.

"I heard all about it," she said. "Stella rang me earlier today."

"But she didn't tell you much you didn't already know," I said. "You could have levelled with me."

Marion Hopcroft shrugged.

"I knew you'd get to the truth, Mike. My father had been killed. That was all that mattered."

"Maybe to you," I said. "You should have been out there today. It looked

307

like the finale of Macbeth. And we got Mackensen killed between us. Remember that. He was an innocent party."

The girl bit her lip. She got up and went over to the balcony, resting her hands on the railing.

"My father was a good man," she said simply.

"So was Mackensen," I told her. "Maybe if I'd known more I'd have been able to save him."

She turned as I got up close to her. She put up her hand and ran it along the edge of my jaw. Her tears were hot and salt on my face as we kissed.

"I've got a lot of explaining to do," I said. "I may lose my licence."

The girl looked at me with brimming eyes.

"I'll go to bat for you, Mike."

"Sure," I said.

I stood away from her and sipped my drink, savouring the malt taste on my tongue and looking at the expensive real estate beyond the balcony.

"Dobbs told me something about The Zetland Method before he died," I said. "He said it was a petrol substitute. But I guess you knew that too."

The girl nodded. There was a strange expression on her face now.

"I knew what it was, Mike. Daddy told me, just the week before he died. He told me something else too. He said he was so disgusted with human nature that no-one should have it."

I stared at her for a long moment, the glass in my hand.

"He destroyed it?" I said incredulously.

Marion Hopcroft nodded.

"He burned the formula down by the swimming pool there. I stood and watched him do it."

I finished off the last of the whisky in one quick gulp.

"Knowing all that, you set me up."

The girl's green eyes looked at me unflinchingly.

"I wanted my father's killer, Mike. I suspected who it might be. But I couldn't prove it. I knew you'd flush him out. What difference would it have made if I'd told you? Murder is murder."

I felt the anger drain out of me.

"Maybe you're right," I said.

"You know I'm right, Mike," she said. "I just let the vultures pick themselves off."

I stood there, thinking of Hopcroft's crumpled figure in the rain; Cranko cartwheeling to death; Mackensen slumped in the Ghost Train car with a wire trace around his neck; Dobbs going down with red stains spreading.

Marion Hopcroft smiled. It was a wry, sad smile.

"He was a good man, Mike."

"Sure he was," I said. "A good man. But was he worth all the pain and death on this case?"

"He was to me," she said.

She gave me a bleak look and turned back to the railing. I left her standing there in the dusk and came away. There wasn't any answer to that. There never is.

Other titles in the Linford Mystery Library:

A GENTEEL LITTLE MURDER
Philip Daniels

Gilbert had a long-cherished plan to murder his wife. When the polished Edward entered the scene Gilbert's attitude was suddenly changed.

DEATH AT THE WEDDING
Madelaine Duke

Dr. Norah North's search for a killer takes her from a wedding to a private hospital.

MURDER FIRST CLASS
Ron Ellis

Will Detective Chief Inspector Glass find the Post Office robbers before the Executioner gets to them?

A FOOT IN THE GRAVE
Bruce Marshall

5		29		53		77	
6		30		54	7/08	78	
7		31		55		79	
8		32		56		80	
9		33	8/05	57		81	
10	1/06	34		58		82	5/15
11		35		59		83	
12		36		60		84	
13		37	11/08	61	7/18	85	
14	5/18	38		62		86	
15		39		63		87	
16		40		64		88	
17		41		65		89	
18		42		66		90	
19		43	12/09	67		91	
20		44	7/10	68		92	
21		45		69		COMMUNITY SERVICES	
22		46	6/09	70			
23		47	2/08	71		NPT/111	
24		48		72			